BORN
BLEEDIN'
LOSERS

BORN
BLEEDIN'
LOSERS

PETER LUFF

BROWN
DOG
BOOKS

Published under licence by Brown Dog Books and The Self-Publishing Partnership, 7 Green Park Station, Bath BA1 1JB

www.selfpublishingpartnership.co.uk

ISBN printed book: 978-1-83952-007-5
ISBN e-book: 978-1-83952-008-2

Cover design by Kevin Rylands
Internal design by Andrew Easton

Printed and bound in the UK

Acknowledgements

I wish to thank Denise for her help and support.

Charlotte and Douglas @ The Self-Publishing Partnership.

Kris @ KJB Marketing.

Finally, I dedicate this book to family and friends
who sadly are no longer with us.

Bless them all.

CHAPTER 1
DAVID HARRIS

Dave Harris woke up startled, as he heard a voice from the radio say, 'Good Morning. It's 7.30. Here is the news.' He'd already been awake once this morning at 6.45 and because it was so cold in his second floor bedsit, he decided to go back to bed, switching on the radio before snuggling under the bedcovers. 'Sod it, must have dozed off,' he said to himself. His mouth was dry, accompanied by a horrible taste, plus a splitting headache, the result of over indulgence the previous evening. Rubbing his tongue along the roof of his mouth and over his teeth he mumbled, 'Yuk. Never again. Why do I do it?' This was his typical response after every hangover, which happened quite frequently. Always regretting taking those extra couple of drinks. The day after the night before, he would swear never to touch another drop of the demon drink. But it didn't last long and as the hangover diminished it wasn't long before a few pints of beer looked appetising yet again.

Outside he could hear a milk float whirling along the street, with crates rocking, bottles rattling, as it passed by below, 'Noisy bastards, why don't yer just bugger off down some other street and give me some peace,' giving him a further reminder of his hangover as he rubbed his forehead. When he put his head above the covers, streams of vapour came from his mouth as his warm breath collided with the cold morning air. He noticed condensation on the window with streak after streak running down the pane forming a puddle on the sill. He lay there for a couple of minutes watching the streaks race one another to the bottom, trying to predict winners. It was a typically cold, crispy November morning with heavy overnight frost.

'Fucking freezing,' he said, as he pulled the bedcover tightly around him, his mind now focused on the forthcoming business, hoping that he had worked out all the details and covered every eventuality.

Dave's full name is David Michael Harris, 26, single, known as 'Hobbly', a result of a very bad motor cycle accident when he was 19 years old. 5'11" tall and weighing approximately 11½ stone, with collar length fair hair and beautiful pale blue eyes, he was considered very good looking and a big hit with the ladies. None more so than the nurses who had cared for him after he'd broken his leg when he was a pillion passenger involved in a very bad accident with a car, where he was catapulted into the air, knocking him unconscious for hours. He sustained a double break of his right leg and spent over a year in hospital, undergoing several operations that left him with a permanent limp. He was idolised by the nurses, not only for courage shown during his long recovery, but also his laid back, happy-go-lucky attitude in adversity. And, not forgetting his good looks, he seemed to have a knack of taking problems, with the occasional setbacks, in his stride, thus gaining some admiration from his elders.

After leaving school at 15 he drifted from one dead-end job to another, unable to find any suitable line that appealed to him. There was *one* job however. If he were ever offered this job, he would have snatched their hand off to accept it. The job? That of a lollipop man. Not because it was the greatest job in the world but the fact that you don't have to start working until you're 65. He was a bit of a jack the lad, with the gift of the gab to go with it. To those who didn't know him well, he may have come across as arrogant or even flash. But this was furthest from the truth to those who really knew him best. He made a few shillings by living off his wits, ducking and diving as one called it, which also included a small amount of crime. He never considered it crime, but I suppose a judge would beg to differ.

He always had a bit of money and was considered one of the best dressed youngsters in town, often wearing the latest trend in fashion. He never married, although he had plenty of offers, but he did get engaged to Sandra on his 24th birthday, sadly only lasting two years. Sandra was a year younger with long blonde hair that ran halfway down her back and, according to Dave, drop dead gorgeous. They were both impetuous; he promised her the earth and in her dream-like state, she willingly accepted it. Sandra easily dismissed reservations from her parents who thought he was a fly-by-night, a bullshitter, and about as good as a wart on the end of your nose. Dave would have needed to win the jackpot on the football pools to finance his unrealistic promises. Firstly, he would buy her a house, not just a house, but a mansion in the countryside with breath-taking scenery, not forgetting tennis court and swimming pool. Perhaps he could change the climate so she could have scorching hot weather all year round too.

Secondly, they'd have children, not just one or two, why not a dozen, perhaps he had a football team in mind, with one sub. And thirdly, work. He would most definitely set up his own business, breeding bloody rabbits presumably. He also promised her huge grounds so she could ride her horses, the children their ponies, with annual racing events. Ascot racecourse comes to mind. Oh the innocence of love! There's nothing wrong in dreaming but in the real world, her infatuation died a little sooner than his; once she finally realised her big mistake she blew him out quicker than a candle. If there was one issue that condemned this relationship above all other, it was that of his friends. Sandra couldn't understand or accept the importance that Dave placed on his friendship with his mates. They consisted of six very close friends.

1) DAVID HARRIS	=	'HOBBLY'
2) DOUGLAS THOMAS	=	'KNOWALL'
3) MAURICE FORD	=	'OILRAG' because of his love for cars
4) TONY BOND	=	'ORANGE' because he was so tight with money, he could peel an orange in his pocket

5) BOB WILSON   =   'MONKEY' self-explanatory really if you saw his face

6) PETER WALKER   =   'LANKEY' was 6'4"

Not exactly the dirty dozen, more like the dirty half dozen. They grew up together in the same neighbourhood attending the same schools, junior as well as senior. An unbreakable bond formed between them, like many others in countless cities and towns up and down the country, when they were young they played, sharing everything with one another. As they grew up they drank, fought the occasional fight, shared the good as well as the bad times together. But more importantly, whenever any one of them was in any trouble the others would gather to give their unquestionable support. Not surprisingly, Sandra wanted him to herself, sod his mates. Despite his constant reassurances, it caused arguments as the relationship deteriorated with the arguments becoming very bitter. It was allowed to fester and, along with other smaller issues, ultimately led to its downfall. It's common among many relationships to have disagreements over friends, such as who favours who. But if you don't accommodate his or her friends you could be on a slippery slope to nowhere.

CHAPTER 2
DOUG THOMAS

'It's half past seven, Doug. Are you getting up?' called Helen. She stood on the bottom stair, listening for some response, but heard nothing.

'It's half past seven, are you getting up?' she repeated, she held her breath not wishing to miss a sound, while listening intensely for some movement. She then heard him moving. Giving a huge sigh, she shouted, 'and I'm not calling you again, you lazy sod.'

This had become a sort of ritual between the pair of them whenever Doug wanted an early call. He would ask his mother to call him at 7 o'clock with no intentions of surfacing much before 7.30-7.45, if at all. On some occasions she would go up to his bedroom and physically shake him just to rouse him from his sleep, leaving her extremely frustrated. She heard footsteps coming from the bedroom. 'Alright mum, keep yer bleedin' hair on, I heard yer,' shouted Doug.

'Well answer, lazy little sod,' she mumbled to herself, as she walked along the hallway, then into the kitchen.

Doug's full name is Douglas Brian Thomas – 26 years old, 5'9" tall weighing 12 stone with dark hair, and single. Affectionately known as 'Knowall' not only because of his excellent general knowledge, but his great understanding of welfare matters. It was known in the 60s affectionately as the 'starving bobs'. A totally useless sod as his mother often called him, who hadn't done a decent day's work since leaving school. On the other hand his grandmother Mavis idolised him. He just couldn't do any wrong according to her and the sun shone out of his backside. His granddad George had a different opinion altogether of his grandson.

'Take the bloody blinkers off woman,' he would tell his wife. He reckoned Doug was without a shadow of doubt one of the laziest buggers he'd ever come across and whenever he got the opportunity he would tell him just what he thought. 'The bloody army would sort you lot out,' you lot referring to Doug and his mates, plus the younger generation in general. 'You're all long-haired layabouts in need of a bloody good scrub. I'm sure you're all allergic to soap. None of you has a decent day's work in you. It's a pity they ever stopped national service, 'cos you buggers wouldn't have lasted 2 minutes. They'd have put you all up against a wall and shot the bloody lot of you. You're born bleedin' losers.'

Mavis thought her hubby was a little jealous and resentful of the younger generation. They had a sort of carefree attitude towards life, and even though many didn't realise it at the time, a whole new world was opening up for them. They were never going to put up with what her generation had to endure. And bloody good luck to them, thought Mavis. They got their news mainly through newspapers, where almost everyone bought or had one delivered daily. Now they had the relatively new phenomenon of television. George wasn't one for change, really. They would watch TV most evenings although George didn't desert his beloved radio altogether. Some programmes they liked, although George would seldom admit to that, some they disliked and he criticised no end. One night they showed a piece about pop music with the pop group The Beatles performing in a field in America, in front of thousands of fans and lots of screaming girls. He pointed at the TV and said, 'There you are, the great unwashed.' Next on, was a piece on another group, The Rolling Stones, with Mick Jagger the lead singer strutting his stuff. That did it. Mavis thought George was going to blow a gasket. 'Call that music? Good god, look at him (Mick Jagger), could you imagine the great big band leader Glen Miller jumping around like that, as if he was being attacked by a fucking swarm of bees.' Mavis told him there wasn't any need to use that language, but she wasn't sure about The Rolling Stones, yet she could see why the youngsters took a liking to the fresh faced Beatles.

'Stupid woman,' he called her.

'Oh, I don't know, seem ok those Liverpublicans.'

'Liverpublicans? You mean Liverpudlians,' he replied.

'No, sure they said they were Liverpublicans,' Mavis replied.

'Liverpudlians you daft bat.' Mavis was further convinced that her husband was envious of these young people and secretly wishing he could be part of it. Where they had peace, pop and plenty of love, he had had big bands, blitz and plenty of bombs. Mavis further annoyed him by suggesting that perhaps Jesus could have been a pop star in his day.

'How do you work that one out?' he asked.

'Well, he had very long hair past his shoulders, good looks and a huge following just like The Beatles and I could imagine him belting one out on the drums.'

'Blasphemous! Blasphemous, you silly woman,' he shouted. It was so easy to wind up her husband.

Doug was unemployed and by George's reckoning, unemployable. Doug's father Brian had died suddenly from a heart attack at the relatively young age of 51, ten years ago, in 1957. Out of adversity and even at the tender age of 16, this could have enabled him to take stock of his life. It would have turned some youngsters into men overnight, eager to prove they were capable of filling the void. But sadly, it made little or no difference and he didn't show any signs of responsibility whatsoever. Brian had tried his best to encourage his son to take a meaningful part in life. He attempted to instil a work ethic, that was so important to him throughout his life, into Doug but unfortunately he had ultimately failed. Mind you the work ethic that he tried to drum into him took a bit of a beating with his very first job.

A friend of his, Bernard, who lived three doors down, saw him one day and inquired what he was doing with his time these days.

'Not a lot,' came the answer.

'Well, why don't come and work with me.'

'Doing what?' asked Doug.

'Painting,' said Bernard.

'Bit of a shit job, enit?' asked Doug.

'Not at all, it's fine. I work at Humphries & Son, down the King's Road,' said Bernard.

'Yeah, I know of it,' replied Doug.

'Well, they got a lot of work at the new housing estate at Binfield, crying out for blokes,' said Bernard.

'Not sure about painting, especially when it gets cold,' said Doug.

'Don't worry about that, do what the other blokes do, get as much work in while the sun shines, save a bit, then have a rest during the winter, easy,' said Bernard before adding, 'got three mates of mine a start only last week.'

Doug thought this Bernard chap was a bit of a dim low, but if he was getting all these people work, then he must be on a bloody good earner, so maybe he'd have to change his opinion. Anyway, it sounded good, the bit about not working in the winter especially. He was offered a start for the following Monday and accepted it.

For the next two months all he did was undercoating, with the experienced painters following behind glossing up. There were rumours that they were beginning to run out of work. Then on a Friday morning they were told to report to the site manager pronto at Humphries & Son's head office. Five of them were summoned and they all had a view on what was about to happen. One thought they should expect a pay rise, another that they might get promotion or a move to another location and one extreme view that they may get an OBE for services rendered.

They were all sacked on the spot, for not knotting the wood (treating hard mass in the new wood before painting). They tried to plead their innocence, but to no avail.

So ended the first lesson: when fresh out of school and in your first job don't always believe what you're told, because some shabby business men will use you, plus screw you and then get rid of you at the drop of a hat when appropriate for them, without blinking an eyelid or even blushing. As for the work ethic, well, the experience left a lasting impression on Doug. Being treated like that went against the grain and his mistrust of business men was everlasting, or was it a convenient excuse for not working?

Doug was ribbed constantly by his mates and even now whenever someone mentions the word painting a cry will go up… 'Get knotted.'

During his school years, Doug showed little or no interest in education despite being given every opportunity, although one bright light came through sport. He became a well-above-average sportsman with a particular liking for cricket, representing the school and county on many occasions. He was also adept at football, becoming an accomplished centre half and a good athlete, excelling in long distance races. However, performances depended largely on whether he could actually be bothered on any one given day. It was as though he had a dislike for success and would press a self-destruct button, just when things were going well,

He didn't show a liking for any subject on the school curriculum. Take Science, for example. He could never understand the point of trying to learn about Science. What bloody good was that to any of us living on a poxy housing estate, because as sure as hell, half the thick buggers couldn't even spell the word science. Can you imagine letting them loose on a Bunsen burner. They banned 80 per cent of Doug's class from ever using it, probably fearing for the safety of the school building and the sanity of the science teacher. It would not have surprised him in the least if once the police got wind of it, they had objected to some reprobates getting hold of such potentially lethal weapons and turning the estate into a war zone. The same went for Maths. What was the point in learning Algebra? It was hardly likely to do you any favours when you were in the queue at the local employment exchange. So Maths didn't appeal to him, just as long as he could add up the pounds, shillings and pence when making a bit on the side with Dave Harris, then fine. Anyway, who needed school to learn? He and his mates frequently went to The Crown public house when they were just 14 years old, where they took turns taking chalks at darts. The locals welcomed them as at least it meant they didn't have to take turns at chalks which most of them hated. The landlord and landlady weren't unduly worried by their age; most looked older anyway, just as long as they behaved themselves and didn't bring any trouble to the premises. Now and again, you had policemen on patrol, checking local pubs, so they needed to keep their heads down. Quite what they would make of Monkey (Bob Wilson) is anyone's guess. Maybe he would have been invited to the next policeman's ball, as part of a cabaret act. Doing chalks gave them the best opportunity to learn to add up and take away, achieving perfection. It also helped in the last year at school, when teacher Mrs Taplin asked Dave and Doug to take over the running of the school tuck shop from Norma White, a prefect, who had decided to step down from doing the job. Mrs Taplin had for some time thought of giving the boys a chance at running the shop, just to see if it made any difference. It was a request from heaven and for these two tealeaves, far too good to refuse. After a month in charge of the tuck shop they were summoned to see Mrs Taplin, in the headmaster's office at 4pm. Panic set in as they wondered what had gone wrong. They knew that they'd had a few bob out of the takings and given away a couple of buns to their mates, as well as eating some themselves, but nothing big. They walked into the headmaster's office expecting to see the headmaster Mr Davis and a few henchmen ready to dish out retribution to two thieving little toe rags. But not so. All they saw was Mrs Taplin sitting in a large leather chair, beaming as they entered.

'Come in boys,' she said. 'I know it's a bit dramatic asking you to come here at this time, but I've been so busy of late, this is the first chance I've had to see you both. I hope it's not too inconvenient for you and I promise not to keep you long.' Relief came over them at the realisation that Armageddon wasn't about to descend on them. 'May I congratulate the pair of you for your magnificent effort over the last month, well it's 32 days to be precise, in the running of our marvellous school tuck shop.' She shuffled some papers on the desk in front of her before picking one up. 'I'm absolutely delighted to inform you that we have never made so much profit in one month from our tuck shop, quite remarkable. What do you think of that, gentlemen?' she asked. Doug mumbled something, but wasn't sure what. Dave stood by the desk absolutely stunned at what he had just heard. 'I have to say it's so nice to see you two boys showing such modesty at what you have achieved, remarkable.'

'Modesty my arse,' thought Dave.

'Now then, I would like the pair of you to go away and consider just how we further improve our tuck shop. We can add a few things. But remember, we cater for a mid-morning break and whatever we do it must not affect the appetite of the lunchtime diners. Do you understand, is that clear?' They both nodded. She's got some chance of that. By the time we're finished the kids will be so full, they'll have a job getting back to the classroom, thought Doug. 'I will talk with you again in, say, seven days, and see if we can work something out between us. That will be all gentlemen once again, thank you.'

They left almost in shock at what they'd just heard and a touch of relief, with some elation at the realisation that 1) they hadn't been rumbled and 2) Christmas had come early. With some changes the tuck shop thrived over the next six months, increasing sales by 50 per cent. Needless to say they also took a substantial increase in takings. Happy days all round. One thing however puzzled them; what did that thieving cow

Norma, prefect and all, get away with before they took over and made a record profit?

CHAPTER 3
OK MEIN FUHRER

Helen opened the front door and saw Dave Harris standing on the doorstep with a holdall on his shoulder.

'Morning, Mrs T. Looking radiant as ever,' said Dave.

'Hello David, do come in, you must be freezing,' replied Helen.

'Thanks. Is your lazy son up and ready for the day ahead?' asked Dave as he wiped his feet on the doormat, before entering the hallway. That's calling the kettle black, thought Helen, leading Dave through to the kitchen where Doug was sitting at a large table.

'Morning toe rag, nice to see you up and about so early,' said Dave as he sat down at the table and placed the holdall down by his side.

'Be in bloody bed if it wasn't for you, Hobbly,' replied Doug.

'Would you like a cup of tea, David?' asked Helen. Dave looked at the kitchen clock on the wall opposite, 8.50. 'Love one, Mrs T. Thank yer. It's OK, we got half an hour before we need to leave,' said Dave.

'Just where are we going, Hobbly?' asked Doug.

'Secret, my man. Secret,' said Dave touching the side of his nose with his finger. Helen placed a cup of tea on the table.

'Help yourself to sugar, David.'

'Sweet enough, Mrs T. Anyway sugar's fattening, need to watch me weight, 'cos no one else will,' said Dave as he patted his stomach.

Just then they heard a tap on the backdoor and in walked Helen's next-door neighbour Barbara.

'It's only me,' called Barbara.

'Just walk in, why don't yer, thought Doug.

'Morning Barbara, can I get you a cup of tea?' said Helen.

'Love one,' replied Barbara before sitting in a chair opposite Dave. 'Morning, Doug. Jesus, you're up early today.'

'Morning Barb, nice to see you yet again,' he replied, shaking his head slightly.

'Is that you, Hobbly?' asked Barbara as she looked across at Dave.

In response he patted his face before replying, 'Yes I think it's me, Barb. I think it's me alright.'

Barbara laughed 'You are a one, Hobbly. How are you?'

'My god yer look more beautiful every time I see yer, Barb,' said Dave.

Barbara blushed a little. 'You are a one,' said Barbara.

'Here's your tea love, help yourself to sugar,' said Helen placing a cup on the table in front of her.

Dave had known Barbara for a number of years, a decent enough woman, not quite a full ticket. Put it this way, when god was dishing out the brains, Barb must have been loitering towards the back of the queue, bless her.

'Tell me, Barbara, how's your husband? I haven't seen him for a while,' asked Helen.

'Gerald's been suffering lately, poor soul. He got very bad sciatica, affects his hip, back, legs and he keeps me awake at night.'

Doug smiled, *Lucky you*, he thought.

'He gets bad headaches, got knee ligament trouble, suffers from tennis elbow, plus he's got flat feet.'

'Christ, anything else?' said Doug.

'Well, yeah. He went to doctors on Monday and was diagnosed with piles,' said Barbara.

'Poor sod,' said Dave.

'I don't understand how he got tennis elbow, Helen, he's never played tennis.'

It was all too much for Dave and Doug as they burst out laughing.

Dave quickly checked himself. 'Sorry, Barb, I didn't mean to laugh,' as Doug ran from the kitchen, still laughing, 'need to go to the toilet, Mum.'

'Poor man, he don't get much luck, does he,' said Helen.

'None at all, he's got to have all his teeth out next week,' said Barbara.

Doug shut the front door behind him, then walked down the path to a gate, before turning to Dave and saying, 'God Barb's a card, Hobbly, don't think I've ever laughed so much, she's definitely not a full shilling,' as he giggled to himself.

'I've thought that for a long time, a penny short of a pound, that's for sure,' said Dave.

As Doug opened the gate then walked towards his car, he noticed Barb's hubby Gerald, waving from his upstairs bedroom window. They both acknowledged him before Doug opened the car door and climbed in, then reached over to open the passenger door. Dave got in, placing the holdall on the car floor between his legs.

'Look at him,' said Doug laughing, as he shut the door. Gerald was still at the window waving. Seeing Gerald, Dave also began to laugh, before saying. 'For fuck's sake, Knowall, the pair of 'em are a loaf short of a picnic.' Doug put a key into the ignition then started it up, first time, which surprised as well as pleased him, considering the overnight frost.

'Can't disagree with that, Hobbly,' said Doug as he adjusted the rear view mirror. 'And, I'll tell yer what, Hobbly, our Gerald's stammer is getting worse, far worse. I saw him last week in Barton's off licence buying cigarettes, right.'

Dave nodded. 'He said to the woman behind the counter, tasty she was, "Can I have 10 wwwww ttttten wwwww." Amazing really, yer could see people in the queue behind him having some sympathy with his predicament. Some were mouthing with him, some encouraging him to spit it out. The shop assistant looked at him as he got more frustrated and trying to anticipate him, interjected with "Ten weights, sir?" [weights being a popular brand]. Still frustrated and shaking his head, Gerald said, "N no, Woodbines." Those behind him cheered. Not because they were piss taking but relief for Gerald and a realisation that they just might get home in time for tea.'

Dave sat, rocking to and fro laughing.

Doug continued. 'When I eventually got out of the shop, gormless was waiting for me. "Well, that was hard work," I said. "Yyyyyy yes," he replied. Fucking hard work trying to have a conversation with him, I'll tell yer. For a start you could do with wearing a mask when facing him, because he don't stop spraying yer. If you could actually turn him into a paint spray, he'd be worth a fucking fortune.'

Dave laughed.

'OK, Mein Fuhrer, where to, Poland?' said Doug. Dave looked at his watch for the umpteenth time. He needed to be in place by 9.40 for it to have any chance of success. 9.10, so all was well.

CHAPTER 4
THE WAIT

Mr Charles White stood at an upstairs window looking down on the frosty grass below that twinkled like little diamonds as the sun shone brightly. A pathway that divided two lawns was footprint free and covered with a thin layer of frost. Beyond the lawns traffic slowly passed, the morning rush hour gradually coming to an end. Exhaust fumes from cars, lorries and buses mingled with the cold morning air.

Charles White was a tall, very elegant man, greying at the temples, immaculately dressed in his tailor made suits, with highly polished shoes. He always had a red carnation in his buttonhole, whenever he wore a suit. He was a 60-year-old married man, with a son James who was fresh out of university, who had for some time been learning the business, ready to take over from his father. Charles had planned his retirement for a long time, having spent 45 years with the company, minus the war years. His father had built it up from nothing, to now employing 23 people in this precision engineering company.

'Brrr,' said Charles as he turned away from the window and

sat down in his swivel chair, which fitted nicely under a large table. 'Certainly looks a cold one this morning, Miss Wise.'

Miss Wise, a spinster, had worked for Charles almost 20 years as a secretary, bookkeeper, tea maker and general dog's body. It may seem archaic in the office, with Mr this, Miss that, but she wouldn't have it any other way. She was old school and would never dream of calling her boss by his Christian name, or vice versa.

'Yes, Mr White. Took a little longer to get into work this morning, slows everything down this type of weather, doesn't it,' replied Miss Wise.

He looked at his watch. 9.10. 'Certainly does,' and with a smile on his face, continued, 'I know the answer already Miss Wise, but are the wage slips and packets done?' (Slips: print-out of salary, hours worked the previous week with deductions. Packet: a small brown envelope with earnings and deductions written on the front, with a pocket to insert money. All wages paid in cash.)

'All ready, Mr White.'

'Well done, another 30 minutes or so and it should be here,' said Charles as the telephone rang.

'OK, Knowall. Take a right and head for Craven Road.'

'Which end, by the post office?' asked Doug.

'No, down the other end.'

'But, that's a dead end,' said Doug.

'Yeah I know. Drive down to the fence, plenty of room to park up. And, while I'm gone, turn the car around,' said Dave.

'All a bit of a mystery, enit,' replied Doug.

'Just drive, Knowall. I'll explain later.'

Dave had spent weeks and many hours checking out this job. He was happy that over this time he had managed to cover every eventuality possible and its potential dangers. He had cancelled this job once, because of days of torrential rain, and couldn't take the risk of looking like a drowned rat. They drove off towards their destination almost in silence. Dave watched as people were going about their daily business in the sunshine, traffic was light in parts, busy in others. They passed by a church as a funeral service had just finished and mourners were about to leave. The majority were black, he'd never seen such a large gathering, and they bowed in respect as the coffin was put back into the hearse.

'They must be going blackberrying,' said Doug.

'You git! Brains of a rocking horse,' said Dave.

Doug stopped at a school crossing. As children crossed he looked over to his right and saw his old school in all its splendour. 'Takes yer back, Hobbly.'

'Yer can say that again, Knowall. Hated it when I was in school, but now I miss it,' replied Dave.

'I suppose it was a lot easier then; we didn't have a care in the world,' said Doug.

'The only care we had was the tuck shop and what we could make out of it,' said Dave.

'Funny that – I found out a lot later that the shit hit the fan when Mrs Taplin found out the true profit, less our fiddling, so we went from heroes to a couple of arseholes in her book. How times have changed.'

They travelled a short distance before turning into Craven Road.

'OK, Knowall, down to the bottom, then drop me off,' said Dave.

'OK, but are you going to explain to me just what this is all about?' asked Doug.

'Tell yer later,' replied Dave.

'Fair enough, seems a bit shady though.'

The car pulled up just short of the fence, as Dave picked up the holdall and placed it on his legs, before checking his watch once again. 9.36.

'Right, Knowall. Turn the motor, then stay, and I mean stay, in the car, don't go on walk abouts, expect me back in 10–15 minutes. Is that clear?'

'Yes Mein Führer,' replied Doug.

With that, holdall in hand and without another word, Dave was gone. He walked through a gap in the fence and once on the other side, he put the holdall down. He had already unzipped it and proceeded to take out items. Firstly a combat jacket, which he put on, followed by some black-rimmed glasses, with clear lenses, a light brown flat cap and, finally, a pair of woollen gloves. He stood on top of a grass verge by a well-worn track leading to a path below. 9.38.

Miss Wise picked up the telephone, as it continued ringing.

'Good Morning, White & Son Engineering. May I help? Yes, certainly. Mr White is expecting your call. I will transfer you through... Mr Barton of Townsend Security,' she whispered.

Charles picked up the extension, 'Good Morning, Mr Barton, may I call you Ronald? OK. Firstly, thank you for calling this morning, Ronald. The main point of consulting with you is because I think we have a need for a complete overhaul in regard to our security.'

He listened to what Ronald had to say. Miss Wise decided to leave the office and head to the kitchen to make tea, the first cup of the day.

'I've picked up on some lapses in our security, Ronald, and I'm not happy. It's good that you have carried out reviews on other companies in our area.'

The conversation continued and a few minutes later Miss Wise was back, carrying two cups of tea and placing one in front of Charles before going back to sit at her desk.

'Interesting conversation, Ronald, very well worth it, I would say. Oh, yes I agree, Ronald. Now then, I've checked my diary and I see I'm completely free next Tuesday morning.' Again, he listened, before saying, 'Excellent, Ronald, 10am. Yes, we must look at everything. Well, thank you very much, Ronald. I'll look forward to meeting with you on Tuesday. Bye now, bye.' He replaced the receiver before taking a sip of tea. 'Very nice man. Miss Wise, can you please make sure you don't book any appointments for me next Tuesday.'

'Yes, very well. I'll make a note of it straight away.'

'I can meet with Mr Barton, then I plan for a round of golf in the afternoon, what do you think of that, Miss Wise?'

'Very good, Mr White, you could do with a little bit of free time,' she replied.

Charles shuffled some papers in front of him, before checking his watch. 9.38.

CHAPTER 5
THE HEIST

Dave slung the holdall over his shoulder, then set off down the wet, muddy track. He hadn't taken more than half a dozen steps when he slipped, falling forward onto his right knee and slowly descending to the bottom of the grass verge. He jumped up quickly, adjusting the holdall on his shoulder, as he composed himself. He could feel his knee throbbing from the impact with the ground. As he looked down he noticed, as well as felt, wet mud on his trousers, from knee to shin. He did his best to quickly rub it off with his gloved left hand and, in doing so, he could feel the knee swelling slightly, the pain increasing. The mud on his trouser leg had diminished, although it still left a heavy stain.

He took off the wet glove and put it in his jacket pocket. With no time to lose he headed towards some traffic lights, his left knee throbbing leaving him with a bigger limp than was normal. On reaching the lights, he noticed they were on red, allowing him to cross, while others came the other way. Once on the other side, he turned left, heading in the direction that he'd just come from. Panic set in, as he caught sight of the security van, so important to the outcome, in the far distance, as he reached his destination. He hurried as much as he could, considering the pain and swelling knee, down the path, leading to a glass-fronted entrance with 'White & Son Engineering' engraved on a glass door. He opened that door with his gloved hard, then entered a reception area. There was no receptionist, long discarded by the company, but the desk and chair remained and, apart from a few cardboard boxes stacked in the corner, it was empty.

Dave placed the holdall on the desk, then turned to his left, opened a door that led to a passageway, that in turn led to the factory. He wedged his foot against the bottom of the door, while he carefully removed a key from the inside. Releasing his foot, the door shut behind him and then locked the door from the outside; he put the key in his pocket.

He went back to the desk. On his right was a flight of stairs leading to two offices, one used by Mr White, the other unused, along with kitchen and toilet. He took off his jacket and cap placing them on the seat of a chair, behind the desk, then took off his glove, putting it in his pocket. From the holdall he took out a long white coat, cleanly pressed, similar to those worn by doctors or dentists, and he put it on. All the factory staff, from machinists to supervisors or managers wore these coats, at the insistence of Mr White. He calculated that appearance was very important to a lasting impression for visitors or potential customers.

Dave had had a fake badge made, with the name Alan Ball

printed on it. He took out a pen and a clipboard that had a piece of paper on it, containing figures with some writing – not of any relevance but for show. Adrenalin quickened as he put the holdall behind the desk, then checked his watch. 9.44. He sat on the desk, clipboard in hand, waiting, and within 20 seconds he saw the security guard walking down the path, two bags in hand; one bag coins, the other notes. He entered reception.

'Morning sir,' said Dave, as the guard placed the bags on the desk, moving Dave in the process.

'Where's Mr Evans?' asked the guard.

'Day off, gone to a funeral, I've stepped in,' replied Dave.

'And, who are you, exactly?'

Tugging on the badge on the breast pocket of the coat, Dave said, 'Alan Ball, sir.'

'God, Alan Ball, now that's a name, England '66 and all that,' said the guard.

'Yeah, Bally,' said Dave.

'Bet you get ribbed a bit,' said the guard.

Just the response that Dave had hoped for and the reason he had selected the name – to take his mind off his job.

'A little, a little,' replied Dave.

'I don't have any notification on my job sheet of any change of receiver,' checking his clipboard.

'I've seen yer before, well not you, but yer mates,' said Dave.

'Have you any identification?' asked the guard.

'In the office,' said Dave.

'Hmm, this is the second time this has happened this month, I need to have a word back at the office, not good enough.'

Now Dave took a big chance. 'If yer have a problem then would yer like me to go and get the boss?' said Dave.

'No, no. That won't be necessary.' He pulled off a piece of paper from the clipboard and said, 'Sign here,' as he laughed. 'Not my money anyway,' he said as he took back the paper. 'Here's a copy for you,' he said.

Before Dave could make any further comment, he was gone, all in less than two minutes from start to finish.

Now he needed to move quickly. He picked up the holdall and placed it on the desk, putting the pen and clipboard in it, followed by the bags of money. He picked up the coat from the chair, then put it on, followed by the cap. He zipped up the holdall, then put it on his shoulder. He took out the glove from his pocket, wiped the handle of the door, then ran it over the desk. Just then he heard the door handle shake, then saw the handle jerk up and down: someone trying to get in from the passageway, as expected.

Time to go, he thought. He then noticed he was still wearing the white coat under his jacket. Sod it, too late to take it off, he thought. A quick glance to make sure he hadn't left anything; then, with the glove in his hand he opened the door, putting it back in his trouser pocket.

Relief washed over him as the cold air circled his face. He hobbled down the path, crossed the road, weaving in and out of a couple of cars until he reached the other side. He climbed the grass verge, avoiding the wet track, with great difficulty ascended it, limping all the way up. At the top, he shouted, 'Yes, I've done it,' and as he turned the corner he punched the air.

CHAPTER 6
REALISATION

Charles finished signing some important papers. He looked at his watch. 9.47.

'Mr Evans should be up very soon, Miss Wise, so get ready.'

'Ready, Mr White,' she replied.

He swivelled the chair round, stood up, then looked out of the window. Quiet out there, he thought, only little traffic, very few people and the sun had dimmed. But, one thing caught his eye. In the distance he noticed a man climbing a grass bank, seemed he was dragging his leg behind him. He wore a jacket, with a white coat underneath. *Wonder if that's one of my men,* he thought.

There was a knock on the door and Charles turned round to see Mr Evans walk in. Slightly out of breath, he asked, 'Have you seen the security guard, Charles?'

'No. Why, Tom?' he replied.

'We may have a problem of some sort,' said Tom.

'Problem of some sort?' asked Charles.

'Yes, something odd occurred this morning.' Tom walked

over to the window and looked out.

'Carry on Tom,' said Charles.

'When I tried the door into reception, it was locked, and the key for the lock was gone. I checked my watch, 9.46.'

'Strange,' said Charles.

'So I had to go round the outside and in through the front door. No sign of the van, no sign of the key either. It's now 9.50 and I don't even know if security's been.'

'What do you mean, exactly?' asked Charles.

'Well. Security van normally arrives between 9.45-9.55, the norm being 9.45. If he gets here early, which is rare, he'll come look for me in the factory. But now, because of the locked door, I'm left in limbo.'

'They wouldn't have aborted the delivery just because of a locked door, they would have come up here,' said Charles.

'Yes, I agree, that's why I asked you when I came in if you'd seen the security guard,' said Tom.

'But, we still have five minutes, let's be positive that it will arrive soon,' said Charles.

They both looked out of the window, hoping for the best, but as time passed, they were merely more confused.

'Tell me, Tom, who's their next delivery, after us?' ased Charles.

'Foster's in Westbridge,' said Tom.

'Then I suggest we call Foster's to see if we really do have a problem, Tom,' said Charles.

'We need to speak to Dave Little,' said Tom.

'OK. Will you call Foster's and try to get Dave Little on the line, please, Miss Wise?' said Charles as he sat down, irritable.

'Yes, very well, Mr White.'

'So where do we stand, Tom?' said Charles.

'I just don't know. The locked door is confusing, as well as worrying,' said Tom.

'Are you thinking what I'm thinking, Tom?'

'And that is?' asked Tom.

'That someone may, somehow, have intercepted the delivery,' said Charles.

CHAPTER 7
THE AFTERMATH

Dave opened the car door and threw the holdall onto the floor, before getting in. It startled Doug, who was having some 40 winks.

'Git, yer made me jump,' he said.

'Let's go, let's go,' said Dave.

As he drove off, Doug looked over at Dave saying, 'What the fuck's that get up?'

Dave laughed as he looked towards the back window, just to assure himself that no one was following, unlikely as it was.

'Jesus, yer look a right wally,' said Doug.

'Keep driving,' replied Dave. He then rested his head on the back of the seat, still buzzing from what he had just done. He shut his eyes, then blew out his cheeks as he recalled events over the last 10 minutes or so. He couldn't believe just how well it had gone, better than he'd ever expected. You'd expect to have one or two dodgy moments, but to go that well – superb.

'What's with the flat cap and glasses, Hobbly? Looks as if you've just got back from racing bloody pigeons.'

'I'll tell yer the story when we get back to the flat,' said Dave. He took off the cap and glasses, then put them in his jacket pocket.

'Yeah, yeah, yer keep saying that, "I'll tell yer later, I'll tell yer later," beginning to sound like a broken record,' said Doug.

'I said I'll give you the full s/p and I will, promise. And, and I can promise summit else... we are in for a fucking good night, tonight, Knowall,' as he laughed out loud, '... yer can bet on that.'

Once they had reached the flat, they walked upstairs to the landing. 'Need a run out,' said Doug, as he walked into a toilet that was shared by other tenants.

Dave carried on to his bedsit, unlocked the door, then entered, putting the holdall on the bed, unzipping it and taking out one of the bags. He undid it, tipping the contents onto the bed – bundles of banknotes. He sat on the chair, taking off both jacket and white coat, while he waited for Doug and, in particular, his reaction to what was on the bed. Doug entered the room.

'I'll tell yer what, yer got some right dirty sods in this', he stopped in his tracks, transfixed at what he was seeing, mouth wide open.

Dave was sat in the chair, looking up at him, waiting for a reaction. With none forthcoming he walked over to the bed, looking down on the money.

'Phew, how much is that?' He looked at Doug then said, 'Not like yer to be tongue-tied, Knowall.'

'What the fuck have yer done?' he replied.

'Little bit of pocket money,' said Dave.

'Pocket money that could clear part of the debt in Africa by the look of it, yer moron,' said Doug.

'Hmm, probably more than I expected.'

'Well, how much did yer get?' asked Doug.

'Dunno, not looked at it yet, have I, Knowall?'

'Yer bastard, I've just realised I'm part of this,' said Doug.

'Part of what?'

'Part of this, if yer get tugged, then I'm an accessory to the crime,' said Doug.

'No, yer not, and that's why I didn't tell yer,' said Dave.

'Well, what fucking difference does that make?' said Doug.

'Don't worry: a) we won't get caught'

Doug interrupted, 'There yer go, yer already implicated me, "We, we won't get caught," yer tosspot,' shouted Doug.

'Go on tell the bloody world, why don't yer, I'm sure everyone would like to know,' said Dave.

'Well, for Christ's sake, I'll do time if we get caught,' said Doug.

'Come on mate, let's have a count up, then we can have a few pints, what do yer say?' said Dave.

'Best thing you've said all day, arsehole.'

'Mr Little from Foster's on the line, Mr White. I'll transfer it through to you,' said Miss Wise.

Charles picked up the receiver. 'Good Morning, Dave. Do you mind if I ask – Have you had your security delivery today?' Charles could feel his heart thumping as he awaited an important answer.

'Yes, we have,' came the reply. Charles nodded his head in the direction of Tom. 'As a matter of fact, Charles, they are still here,' said Dave.

Really surprised and not expecting to hear that, Charles asked, 'Would it be possible to speak with the person who's doing the delivery?'

'I'll see if he's available to speak; give me a minute,' replied Dave.

'Has he been?' asked Tom.

'Afraid so.'

'Damn,' replied Tom.

'Hello again, I've got John here. I've told him who you are, so I'll hand the phone over to him, Charles.'

'OK, thank you, Dave.'

'Good morning, Charles, John speaking.'

'Hello, John, can you please tell me, did you deliver to White & Son Engineering, this morning?'

'Yes, we did.'

Now it hit home and Charles gave out a sigh, before responding. 'Who accepted the delivery, John?'

'Well, it wasn't your normal man, as I recall – Mr Evans,' said John.

'Then who was it?' replied Charles.

'Mr Alan Ball,' said John.

'But we don't have a Mr Alan Ball among our workforce,' said Charles.

Now the penny dropped for John; had he dropped a bollock and how was he going to avoid any blame.

'Well, it was Alan Ball,' said John.

'How do you know that?' asked Charles.

'Well, he had a name badge and also an identification pass for your company.' He had to lie about the identification pass to cover his own back.

'Very well, John. Please can you treat our conversation in the strictest of confidence and under no circumstances repeat it to anyone.'

'I can assure you, Charles, I will not repeat this conversation to anyone,' said John.

'Very good. This will now become a police matter and further talks will be held, do you understand, John?'

'Yes, of course,' replied John.

'Good, now can you put Dave back on?' said Charles.

'Hello, Charles.'

'Dave, I can't go into detail, but I will give you a call in a few days to explain.'

'That's fine,' said Dave.

'Thank you Dave,' as he put the phone down. 'Seems we have a rogue worker in our midst… I don't think,' said Charles.

'So it was intercepted,' said an ashen-faced Tom.

'Yes. Now it's time for the police to investigate.'

Charles had considered all outcomes in this scenario and had decided to call a friend, Detective Dennis Milne.

'Before I call the police, can I say to both of you, nothing must be said to anyone outside this room, for the time being.

Also, Tom, I will later discuss with you about the lost money and what we can do about staff wages. OK? Miss Wise, I'll give you a number shortly. So will you call it for me…?'

'Yes, Mr White.'

A few minutes later Charles was talking to detective Milne. 'Morning Dennis, how are you?' asked Charles.

'I'm fine, nice to hear from you. Look Dennis I have a problem here'

Dennis interrupted. 'By here, you mean the engineering company?'

'Yes, sorry. I'll give you a rough outline; we have had a theft here this morning and a large amount of money taken.'

'Right, Charles. Go through the normal channels on reporting this and I will intervene as soon as possible.'

'We will make that call, Dennis.'

'OK, Charles, see you later, bye.'

Later turned out to be two hours later, when Detective Milne walked through the door.

'Good to see you, Charles.'

'Would have been better under different circumstances,' said Charles.

'Quite so,' replied Dennis.

'No doubt you've been briefed,' said Charles.

'Yes. I will have to speak to Mr Evans, then the security guard, to get their view,' said Dennis. He took out a file. 'I'll start with you, Charles. Tell me what you know.'

'I'm dumbfounded, really.'

'Don't take this the wrong way. Is there anyone in your

workforce who could have pulled this off, Charles?'

'Certainly not,' said Charles.

'Need to explore all avenues, was there anything unusual that you can recall?'

'There's one thing that's bugging me. Presumably at around the time of the theft I looked out of the window, awaiting delivery, when I saw a man, climbing the bank over there, wearing a jacket, with a white coat underneath. I did think at the time it was one of my men.'

'That's interesting, we can delve into that. Anything else?' asked Dennis.

'He was too far away to give you an accurate description, but I think he had a limp.'

'A limp,' said Dennis.

'Well, yes. Although he had a limp I didn't see him fall.' They stood by the window looking out.

'Show me where you saw him,' asked Dennis. Charles pointed to the grass verge in the distance. 'Did he walk up that track and up to that fence?'

'He walked up to the fence, but on the grass.'

'Anything else, Charles?'

'No, I don't think so.'

He opened the file and made a few notes. 'I'll leave my case on your desk, because I need to speak with Mr Evans. Show me the way, Charles.'

'One more thing, Dennis, the man was carrying a holdall, on his shoulder,' said Charles.

CHAPTER 8
LET'S HAVE A DRINK

'Sod it, ballsed up again, keep miscounting the money,' said Doug. They had lined up the notes in bundles on the coffee table. 'Do you reckon that the security company have the serial numbers for these notes?' he asked.

'Dunno, never thought of that, what do yer think?' replied Dave.

'Dunno either. Reckon they could take numbers on big denominations, but not on pounds or ten bobs. Who knows?' said Doug.

'Bollocks, I never gave it a thought. Good job yer said that, well done, Knowall.'

'Yer have to find out, Hobbly.'

'Yeah, I reckon twinkle-toes will know,' said Dave.

'Right, Knowall. Take a couple of pound notes and a few ten bob notes. I'll do the same.' And, taking out the other bag from the holdall and plonking it on the table, he said to Doug, 'Undo the bag and take out some coins, put a few on the table for me.'

'Right,' said Dave, as he took a few notes from the table.

'Then can yer bag up the rest of the notes for me, mate? I'm gonna get changed.'   While he was doing the bagging up, Doug asked, 'How did this theft come about?'

'Goes back a long way. I noticed, one day, the security van deliver money to Whites, when I was passing by. So it got me thinking. The next week, same time, I took another look and noticed the guard hand over some bags to someone inside. And the thing that struck me was, the guard was in and out in less than a minute. So, I got a friend of mine, who will remain nameless, to do a reconnaissance job, where access to the premises were gained with little effort. The rest is history, really. Now all I need to do is weigh 'em in a few bob.'

'Sounds straightforward, but yer must have some bottle to do it, I'd have been crapping myself,' said Doug.

'Well, adrenalin kicks in and takes over. If yer keep to the plan, then yer have a chance; deviate from it, then yer have a chance of ballsing it up.'

'Still think yer got some bottle,' said Doug.

'I dunno, but I did make one mistake. I forgot to take the white coat off before I left. Only a small mistake, but still a charger, nonetheless.

Dave washed, shaved and changed.

'Right, Knowall, I think I'll put those bags in the bottom of that wardrobe over there,' pointing to it. 'At some point, I need to get rid of the white coat, glasses, cap and gloves, all incriminating evidence.' Dave saw that Doug had put away the bags. 'So if you're ready, let's go,' as he picked up coins from the table.

'Yeah, that's all right.' They drove off. 'Wonder what reaction the governor of Whites had to the theft,' said Doug.

'Pissed right off, I should think,' replied Dave.

'Bet he is and his workers, they must be right cheesed off, poor sods, won't even get paid or have enough for a pint,' said Doug.

'What yer trying to do, make me feel guilty?'

'Some fucking chance of that, Knowall,' said Dave.

'By the way, who was it?' asked Doug.

'Who was what?' replied Dave.

'Who was yer mate on the recce?' asked Doug.

'Can't say,' said Dave.

'It wasn't any of our little group on the Whites job, was it. So who was he?' asked Doug.

'Took yer time asking the question, Knowall,' said Dave.

'Christ's sake, so who was he, who?' said Doug.

'It was… MRS Unnamed. Doug, let's be careful how we spend our bit of money; don't go over the top in case people notice, and let's not say anything about this morning.'

'What do yer think I am?' said Doug.

They entered The Crown pub through a door that led to a public bar, one of two separate rooms. The first bar had tables and chairs, darts board, and a long counter. To the left of this counter was a door leading to a bottle and jug, plus saloon bar. The bottle and jug was a small narrow room, where you could enter from the street to get a takeaway of sorts. They had a serving hatch and a couple of stools, where mainly little old dears would spend time sipping their bottle of stout, out of the way of, or in avoidance of, other punters. Others came in with large cylindrical jugs with handles to get them filled with beer, along with a couple of stout, ready for their hard-working husbands to drink along with dinner.

'Morning, chaps, the usual?' asked Len, the landlord.

'All right, Len? Yeah, two pints of bitter,' said Dave.

Doug looked up at the clock above. 12.10. 'Morning Len,' he said.

'Not like you to come in Thursday lunchtime,' said Len.

'Well, thought we'd come in for a change,' replied Dave.

'I just saw Roger when we were coming in here – very smart,' said Doug.

'Well, funny really. He came in earlier, wearing a very smart blue pinstriped suit; with shirt, tie, highly polished shoes. I swear you could see your face in them. He looked immaculate and, to top it off, he wore a little red handkerchief in his top pocket. So I walked down from the saloon bar when I saw him standing at the counter waiting to be served. "Dustbin's round the back, mate," I said to him and walked away. Then I heard him say, "It's me, it's me." "Oh, Sorry, Roger didn't recognise you."'

They all laughed as he placed the pints on the counter. Dave gave him a ten bob note.

Len took the money then said, 'Couple of your mates in the other bar.'

Dave took his change and followed Doug through a door into a second room of the public bar. This room had a bar billiards table near a window, a door that led to the street, tables and chairs and long bench seating on one wall. Opposite the window ran a long counter and to the right, a door to the men's toilet.

'Afternoon, yer two reprobates,' said Dave.

'And what are you two doing here?' asked Tony.

They sat down on the bench opposite with Tony Bond, 'Orange', and Bob Wilson, 'Monkey'. This was the lads' regular spot where, during drinking sessions, they would discuss the weather, sport, politics, sex – not in that particular order.

'We've popped in for a pint, what yer bin up to?' asked Dave.

'I got a few days off, first day off in five weeks,' said Bob.

'Bully for you,' said Tony.

Ethel, the pub clearer, came from the outside door into the public bar.

'Afternoon boys,' she said, as she scurried through to the other bar.

'Afternoon Ethel,' they shouted in unison.

'Yer a bit of a ladies' man, Tony. Tell me, would yer give 'er one?' asked Doug.   'No, not my type,' replied Tony, as he shook his head.

'Well, she's deaf as a post, so she wouldn't hear yer farting, when you're on top,' replied Doug.

'That's true Tony, he has a point, 'cos the way yer keep blowing off, sometimes it sounds like a machine gun's going off,' said Dave.

'He's at it again, listen,' said Doug.

'Bollocks,' said Tony.

'Afternoon lads, coarse as ever,' said Glenda, the landlady.

Beautiful woman, lovely personality and gorgeous legs to go with it.

'Afternoon C,' said Dave.

She wiped a pint glass. 'Unusual for you lads to come in at lunch time,' said Glenda.

'Only came in to see you, C,' said Tony.

'Oh, that's nice... bullshitter,' said Glenda. All the others cheered. 'Where's the other two?' asked Glenda.

'The other two lemons are working,' said Doug.

'Hope to see you and them tonight; we have women's darts,' said Glenda as she walked away.

'I've got to come in tonight, got to get cigarettes off Eric,' said Tony.

'Get loads of cheap gear in this boozer?' asked Bob.

'Not much,' said Tony.

'I can name at least five,' said Dave.

'Not sure you can,' replied Tony, adding, 'that's not counting the fags, right.' 'Yer got...' said Dave, 'One. Alex gets clothes cheap. Two. Ray gets meat cheap. Three. Thomas gets spirits cheap. Four. Larry gets shoes cheap. Five. Dirty Doris... is... cheap!'

'You are a tosser, Dave,' said Tony.

'Come on, yer round, Doug, I don't expect Orange to get them in, tight-fisted git,' said Dave.

'What time is it?' asked Tony.

'12.45,' said Doug.

'Time I wasn't here,' replied Tony.

'Fancy a thrashing, Monkey?' asked Dave, pointing to the billiard table.

CHAPTER 9
DETECTIVE MILNE

Tom entered the office. 'Detective Milne said he would see you about 3.30, Charles.'

'That's fine,' Charles replied.

'Can I get you both a cup of tea?' asked Miss Wise.

'Yes, please,' replied Charles.

Tom went over to the window and looked out while Charles got out of his swivel chair to join him.

'It keeps going over and over in your head, doesn't it, Charles,' said Tom.

'Certainly does,' replied Charles.

Tom pointed. 'Is that detective Milne over there on top of that grass verge?'

'I do believe it is,' said Charles as he saw Dennis, hands on hips looking down, as he spoke to someone. 'Did you speak with Dennis at any length?'

'I did and I have this impression that he thinks it's an inside job; don't ask me why, but I just do,' said Tom.

'Don't be silly,' replied Charles.

'Well, it seems that it was carried out with ease, without any real obstacles to overcome,' said Tom.

'Please, don't I know that, my security review should have taken place long ago. Anyway, that's another matter,' said Charles.

'The one big question that has baffled all of us is the key and who took it,' said Tom.

'Here you are, Mr White,' as Miss Wise placed two cups on the table.

'Thank you, take a seat, Tom,' replied Charles.

Tom sat down opposite Charles, pulling one cup towards himself and the other in the direction of Charles.

'I don't know what the answer is,' said Charles.

'Well, if you were a detective investigating this, then it could well look like an inside job.'

'Yes, I agree,' replied Charles.

'Something else to complicate it further, was it a two-man job,' said Tom.

'You know, I never thought of that,' said Charles.

'It is possible for someone to intercept the money, then pass it over to someone else,' said Tom.

'But, then the interceptor could be recognised later by the guard,' said Charles.

'That's possible I suppose,' replied Tom.

'Better leave it to the pros,' said Charles, as he sipped his tea. 'Now then, Tom. I think we'll have to call a meeting to explain to staff about lost wages.'

'Just what can we do?' asked Tom.

'Tomorrow's Friday, followed by the weekend. I see no way of getting the money replaced before next week. I'm looking at, out of my own bank account, funding twenty-five per cent of each man's wage. I think they would appreciate that gesture. I will have to make sure I do this after I speak with Dennis, so everything is completed by tomorrow lunchtime. Miss Wise is working out the sum needed. Drink our tea, then we will take on the unenviable task,' said Charles giving a glance at his watch. 2.30.

'Last orders gents please,' said Len.

'Half two already,' said Dave. 'Where yer going this afternoon, Bob?'

'Got to go with Mum, doctor's appointment.'

'Nothing serious I hope?' said Doug.

'No, back problems again,' replied Bob.

'That's carrying yer lot about for all these years,' said Dave.

'She had eight kids, didn't she Monkey?' said Doug.

'Yeah,' said Bob.

'Jesus, eight kids, must have spent more time at maternity than some of the midwifes,' said Dave.

'Must have a ward named after her,' said Doug.

'Drink up, please, let's have your glasses,' said Len. 'Don't forget Sunday, lads. Football. Needle match, Crown v Millers,' he pointed to Dave. 'Are you going?'

'Yes. Are you going, Knowall?'

'Yes. Are you going, Monkey?'

'No, no.'

'What do you mean, "No"?' replied Len.

'Can't go,' replied Bob.

'Can't let the side down,' Doug said.

'Len's sister Julie's moved into her new home, hubby Winston has invited us all round for tea.'

'But you wouldn't get them all seated,' said Doug.

'Well, he's got a massive table; seats fourteen apparently.'

'That's a big "chimps tea party",' said Len. 'Drink up, please.'

'Bit below the belt,' said Doug.

'Was a bit,' said Dave. 'Yer know what, Knowall, I fancy going down to Lyon's cafe this afternoon, have a bit of the "Kate and Sydney". Beautiful,' said Dave.

'Have some of that,' replied Doug. They placed the empty glasses on the bar, 'Catch yer later, Len,' said Doug.

'Yeah, see you tonight,' said Bob.

'Thanks lads,' replied Len.

They headed to Lyon's less than five minutes' away.

'Could eat a horse,' said Doug.

'Hope we don't get served that,' replied Dave. 'Last time I visited Lyon's there was a bit of a row. Dozey Daisy was in one of her weird moods. Poor cow behind the counter just couldn't do anything right for Dozey. I don't think anyone on this planet could have tried, cajoled or attempted to meet Daisy's needs. I was sat watching and trust me, Dave, there was no way that I would have put up with that. She must have been on the same wavelength, because she'd had enough, an' snapped. She broke all customer service etiquette, by telling Daisy to —eff off.'

'Dozey Daisy has always been a bit of a psycho,' said Dave.

'Yep, when Daisy had the front to object, the assistant warned her, "if you so much as moan once more you'll be wearing that lunch on your fucking head," before storming out. I thought, fair play to you, love.'

'And, would she have done it?' asked Dave.

'The look in her eyes told me she would definitely have done it, with extra helping.'

They were soon sitting down enjoying a steak and kidney pie, chips and peas, with gravy. Doug looked around. No one within earshot. 'How do yer think the police investigating is going?' he asked.

'I wondered about that earlier, it's a tricky one.'

'How do yer mean?' asked Doug.

'Well, they have a few suspects, really. I could not believe they didn't have one camera recording it. So that must have angered the police.'

'Certainly would have made my job harder, may not even have attempted it. So now I don't see how they can rule anything out, for the time being.'

'Yer certainly gave them something to think about, Hobbly,' said Doug.

'Let's hope so,' replied Dave.

Detective Milne entered the office.

'Hello Charles, Miss Wise.' Both acknowledged him. 'I'll give you an update. Charles, is it OK to speak in front of Miss Wise?'

'Miss Wise is one hundred per cent reliable, so feel free to speak in front of her.'

'I thought that would be the case. Firstly, Charles, I don't recall ever coming across such a pathetic lack of security. Not a single camera, not even a dummy, not a single photo of the intruder. Quite astonishing. But, then you're aware of that.'

'I certainly am, Dennis.'

'You will not like this, but it must be said. I hold my fiercest criticism for Mr Evans. He has shown an astonishing lack of understanding of the concept of security. A total lack of awareness, anticipation or prevention, everything you would expect from him in those circumstances.'

'That's a little harsh,' said Charles.

'Not one bit, Charles. Here's just one example. He told me himself, should the security guard arrive early and he wasn't there waiting to greet him, no problem, he was to go find him in the factory.'

'Hmm,' muttered Charles.

'No problem? I would say *big* problem. Anticipation, Charles. If security personnel can go looking around the factory, willy nilly, then so can anyone else. Had he for one minute considered the security aspects he certainly would have seen holes appearing like a sieve. None of that happened.'

'I get your point, Dennis.'

'I spoke with John, the guard, on the telephone. He is coming into the station tomorrow morning; show him a few mug shots, etc. He gave a brief description of the interceptor. Five foot ten or eleven, around twelve stone, mid-twenties, between fair and mousy brown hair, whatever that means.

It's very disappointing. We need to improve on that. He wore black-rimmed glasses. No distinguishable features that he can recall. So, as you can see, Charles, a lot to work on with John.'

'He gave me a little snippet of information. The intruder wore a pair of grey trousers; he noticed a light smearing of a sandy-coloured substance on the knee and down the shin.'

'Charles, you mentioned a man climbing the bank, who seemed to be limping, but didn't see him fall.'

'Correct, I also thought it could have been one of my men,' said Charles.

'John couldn't confirm or deny if the man had a limp. I visited that grass verge.'

'Yes, we saw you. It's quite steep.'

'Could that person you saw, and John encountered, be the same? If so, then we must consider that he came and went via the grass verge, with the possibility of falling down the muddy track on his way here, hence the smear on the trousers.'

'Interesting,' said Charles.

'Beyond that fence is Craven Road. So, it may, I emphasise, *may* give us our first clue. Did he park a car or any other transport in Craven Road? Did he have an accomplice who dropped him off and waited for his return? Did he work alone? Did he arrive on foot and leave the same way? I need foot soldiers to do a little digging and come up with some sightings of our mystery man, to or from this place.'

'Well, I would suggest some progress, Dennis.'

'Maybe I need more from John. I'll work on him tomorrow.'

Tom knocked on the door and entered. 'How's it going

Detective Milne?' ask Tom.

'Slow, Tom, but we will get there.'

'Do you want me, Tom?'

'Yes, Charles,' replied Tom. 'It's four o'clock, I'm reminding you about the bank.'

'Yes, Tom, I managed to talk with Michael earlier this afternoon. Dennis, I've arranged or will arrange a plan with my bank to pay twenty-five per cent of the staff's wages. No objection, I trust?' said Charles.

'No, why should I?' replied Dennis.

'Just checking.'

'So, is it all systems go?' said Tom.

'Not yet. Miss Wise will give me a total shortly and I will inform Michael the bank manager, so he can arrange for the money to be in his bank by 11.30 tomorrow.'

'As long as you're not having it delivered, Charles,' said Dennis, smiling.

'No, those days are over, Dennis. I will need two of our staff to accompany me to the bank. Once we get the money, we'll come back here, where Miss Wise will make up the wages.'

'Should any of the staff ask, what time can they expect the wage, roughly?' asked Tom.

'I would say 2.30,' replied Charles.

'A busy day tomorrow all round,' Dennis said. 'Friday 13th. I hope it will be an uneventful day for you, Charles, but a truly fruitful one for me.'

CHAPTER 10
THE FIRE

Friday 13th, some people refuse to go out that day. Bad luck? Another cold crispy morning, with a heavy overnight frost. A car passed by, splashing a puddle in the kerb, the remnant of the ice, which Doug did well to narrowly avoid.

'Git,' shouted Doug. 'How come I always get it, when it's never worth having?'

'What time did yer say you'd be there?' inquired Dave.

'I didn't, but around eleven o'clock.'

'What does she want yer for?' asked Dave.

'Questions, questions. Look, me mum said Aunt Vi wanted to see me in the morning sometime, she didn't know why, what for, or even care.'

'Wow, sounds like she don't like yer aunt Vi, much,' said Dave.

'No, not much love lost between them,' said Doug.

'Stop a minute,' said Dave as he bent down to rub his leg.

'Is it giving you some stick?' asked Doug.

'Yeah, may have to go and see the quack, find out what he

thinks,' replied Dave.

'Think yer should, noticed yer limp's getting worse,' said Doug.

'Anyway, go on,' said Dave.

'Where were we? Oh yeah, Aunt Vi's a big woman, more to share around, she says, and she literally does. She's always had big tits, Dave, enormous. When I was about 13, I went to a wedding and she was there. When she saw me, she headed straight in my direction, "Is that you Douglas, it's not little Douglas, is it? My, haven't you grown up. Come here, give us a hug," she said. God, it was like being smothered by a pair of pillows. I was fighting for air, while she was loving it. I imagined those weirdos down at the Odeon cinema every night would have been in heaven getting attacked by a huge pair of knockers like that. Total bliss for them. I've always been wary, ever since, of breasts.'

'What, do yer break out in a sweat every time yer get near a pair of big knockers?' said Dave.

'I jump when there's a knock on the door,' replied Doug. 'Anyway, me mum reckons she's a tart and a bag of fleas,' said Doug.

'Dunno, sounds to me that she's a sort of free spirit,' said Dave.

'Free spirit's right. Vodka, brandy, whiskey, gin, she'll drink it, just as long as someone's buying it.'

They crossed the road, then turned the corner, before crossing again. After walking a little way they noticed a woman waving her arms, pointing and wailing. Nobody else was around; the street was empty of people by the look of it. As they edged nearer, they could see the front door wide open, with the woman standing by the kerb and just six feet away from the door. They were aware of the layout of these types of terraced houses. Parlour, living room, kitchen, scullery, narrow staircase, two bedrooms plus box room. They also had a coal shed, next to a toilet, very primitive, where the occupant would cut up newspapers into squares, before putting them on a hook, ready for use – no such luxury as toilet rolls. The man of the house spent ages in the toilet reading snippets of last week's news. You had a mangle for wringing out wet laundry. A tin bath hung from a wall and was brought into the scullery at bath times. A boiler was used to heat the water, ready for as many as six kids to bathe – that's primitive.

Once they reached the woman they could see she was extremely agitated, pummelling her head with her fist, in between pointing to the upstairs window. 'What's the problem?' asked Dave.

'What did she say?' asked Doug.

'Dunno, she's foreign, I think,' replied Dave.

'Need to take a look,' said Doug, as they stepped onto the doorstep. As they moved cautiously into the passage, Dave heard the faint sound of an alarm.

'Where's that coming from?' he asked.

'Not really sure,' replied Doug.

'Right, I reckon someone must be in here, somewhere. Let's start looking. I'll check in here, can yer check the living room and scullery?' Dave opened the door to the parlour and walked in, no sign of anyone, just a settee, with other pieces of furniture. He returned to the passage, just as Doug came through the living room.

'No sign of anyone,' he said.

'Yer sure no one's lying injured?' said Dave.

'No, there's no one through there,' replied Doug.

'Let's try upstairs,' said Dave. As they ascended the stairs, the sound of the alarm grew increasingly loud as they reached the top. They could not go any further forward at the top, because of a wall, only left or right were options. It became obvious that the alarm came from behind the door.

'Can't smell any smoke,' said Dave.

'No, no heat either,' as Doug felt the door.

'I'll take the front; take the back, Knowall.'

They both opened their doors gingerly, as they looked behind the doors. 'Can't see any dangers,' shouted Doug.

'Nor me,' replied Dave, as he walked into the room. He picked up an alarm clock and switched it off. He heard the whimpering sound of a baby, then saw a cot in the corner of the room. He walked round a double bed, past a window and stood at the bottom of the cot. 'See if the woman is still outside, Knowall,' said Dave.

'OK,' said Doug. As he walked past the bed to a window Dave looked down on a seven-month-old girl who, as soon as she saw him, started smiling, gurgling and kicking her legs in the air.

'Hello, young one,' said Dave.

'Yeah, she's still at it,' said Doug.

'Dunno why she is acting like this, do you?' asked Dave, 'Unless it was the alarm that frightened her.'

'Take a look at this lot,' said Doug. In the alcove of a chimney breast were piles and piles of newspapers and a stack of cardboard boxes, also an electric fire giving out some heat.

'Do yer think they're old papers that may be worth a bit of money?' asked Dave.

'Maybe, let me have a look, then I can ferret in those boxes, just make sure we're not disturbed,' said Doug. As he stretched over to look at one of the papers, his foot tangled with the lead from the fire and knocked it onto the floor. Within seconds the very dry newspapers ignited and burst into flames. 'Get out, get out,' shouted Doug. Dave rushed to the cot. 'Yer dozey bastard,' he shouted, as he bent over, picking up the child. A sheet of flames flashed across the alcove, catching the curtains in the process.

'Get out, get out,' shouted Doug again. Dave could see his exit was blocked by the fire at the window, so he crawled across the bed, clutching the child tightly. Doug helped them off the bed. 'Are you OK?' he asked.

'Yeah, let's get out.' The fire began to take hold, flames shooting up and out of the window. They rushed down the stairs and along the passage and straight out of the door onto the pavement. Doug looked up and saw the flames coming from a gap above the window; glass began to crack.

'Quick, get to the other side of the road.'

Doug grabbed the arm of the woman, who had her arms outstretched in anticipation of receiving her child. People came out of the houses from up and down the street. The young child was handed over to a grateful mother, who cuddled the girl, while patting the face of Dave in a gesture of gratitude. One man knocked on the adjacent door to warn occupants of the danger above. Glass shattered, smoke blew out of the opening, as particles of burning curtains fell to the ground. A woman came up to Doug and hugged him; her husband shook his hand.

Another went to Dave and said, 'You are a hero young man; you saved that child, thank God.'

Doug looked at Dave and vice versa, in total bewilderment. Small groups of people stood around chatting taking the odd glance in their direction.

Dave pulled Doug to one side. 'Jesus, what have we done?' asked Dave.

'Sorry, I didn't mean it,' replied Doug. They could hear fire engines in the distance. 'Shall we leg it?' said Doug.

Dave felt a hand on his shoulder. 'Hello sir,' he heard as he turned to see a policeman. 'I understand you've been in the building to rescue a child, are you able to tell me if any other persons are in the building?'

'Nobody's in the house,' said Dave.

'How can you be so sure?' asked the policeman.

'We searched the rooms on our way out,' replied Dave.

'Yeah that's right,' said Doug.

'Ok, that's fine, stay here. I'll have a word shortly. I must tell the fireman they have the all clear regarding people inside.'

Other people congratulated them, shook hands, kissed them.

Oh, God, this is getting out of hand, thought Dave. 'Shall we get lost?'

Doug saw the fire engine pull up; fire men alighted and went in all directions. There was now a sizeable crowd gathered, creating a sort of jovial atmosphere. The crowd applauded, then cheered as firemen went about their business.

'Bring in the clowns why don't you? Can't stand much more of this, Hobbly,' said Doug.

'No, we'll soon have someone selling hats, balloons and ice creams,' said Dave. Five minutes later and out of the corner of his eye, Doug saw the policeman accompanied by a fire officer, approaching. 'Ah shit, Hobbly,' said Doug.

'Hello lads, we'll soon have this fire under control.'

Again, someone patted Doug on the back, 'Good on you, mate,' someone said.

'You're getting a good response from these people, and rightly so,' said the policeman. 'Thank you both for giving us some useful information regarding the fire and dispelling the fear of trapped people.' An ambulance arrived to the sound of cheers and clapping. 'Are either of you in need of medical treatment? Only the officer here saw you limping earlier,' said the fire officer.

'No, we are both fine,' said Dave. Just then a camera clicked several times.

'Do you mind, trying to conduct a conversation,' said the policeman.

Dave's heart sank. *That's all we need, why didn't we clear off when we had the chance,* he thought.

'These press boys won't give up, get used to it lads,' said the fire officer. 'Can I ask you about the fire?' asked the officer as he pulled them to one side.

A fireman approached, 'Sir, we have it under control; the damage was mainly contained to the bedroom, with smoke damage on the stairs.'

'OK, thank you,' said the fire officer before continuing, 'How do you think the fire started?'

'With an electric heater igniting bundles of newspapers and cardboard boxes,' said Dave.

'Lethal mix,' said the officer. 'Was it alight when you entered the room?'

'It had just caught light, so we grabbed the child, as the flames engulfed the alcove,' said Doug.

'Where was the electric fire?'

'Stood in front of the papers, but on the way out of the room I stumbled over the lead, it knocked the fire into the papers, although it was already well alight.'

'That's fine, I'll get to take a look later.' He turned to the policeman. 'Any questions, officer?'

'I will need a statement in due course.'

'Well, thank you gentlemen, I will leave you to the vultures,' said a smiling fire officer, as he walked away with the policeman.

'Fuck's sake, Doug, what are we in for?'

Again, they heard click, click, then saw a pressman. 'Smile lads, smile. It's the *Daily Echo.*'

Oh God, thought Doug.

'You'll be on the front tomorrow, local heroes, what a story!

Is it right you went into an inferno and rescued the sprat? That takes some bollocks. Did you only just make it out?' Doug looked at Dave in disbelief, both aware of the way this was going, once this moron had finished. 'Let's have the story, lads,' asked the pressman.

'Later,' said Dave.

'Got to write something, boys.'

'Write what you like and I'm sure yer will,' said Doug. They both walked through the crowd, people still slapping them on the back, others clapping them. They reached the policeman.

'Do you need us for anything?' asked Dave.

'Why do you want to get away, lads?' Away from Sandy the pressman?' asked the officer.

'Yeah,' said Doug.

'Leave your name, address and contact number,' he gave them a notebook and pen. 'Can you make it down to the station later this afternoon? Ask for P.C. Mellor. I'll be there is a couple of hours.'

'Here yer are, constable, names, address. We put his contact number down, is that OK?' said Dave.

'Yes, fine. Thanks lad.' He took the notebook.

'Let's get going,' said Dave.

'Where's the pressman?' asked Doug.

'Dunno, can't see him,' said Dave. They came face to face with the woman and child who were being led to an ambulance, accompanied by a neighbour who had been caring for them since leaving the fire. They stopped to look inside the ambulance.

'Are they OK?' asked Doug.

'We are taking the baby in, just as a precaution, get her checked over, but she'll be fine.'

'How's the mother?' asked Dave.

'She's OK, doesn't understand English, so it's been difficult getting through to her.' Click, click, click, they heard.

'Not you again,' said Doug. Standing there was Sandy, a short-tempered, ginger-haired Scot with a bushy beard. He was never seen without his beloved tartan beret, long tartan scarf, with round lens glasses, perilously perched on the end of his nose.

'How about a nice picture of you two, holding the baby? Perfect,' said Sandy. The ambulance man closed the door abruptly. 'Hmm, how about a picture of you two, in front of the fire, very dramatic, make a great splash in tomorrow's *Echo*.'

Doug looked over towards the fire, which had almost been extinguished with just the odd plume of smoke escaping from the window.

'What do yer think, Hobbly, shall we give him a photo and be done with it?' said Doug.

'He still won't leave yer alone,' replied Dave.

'Listen, er, what's yer name...'

'Sandy.'

'Right, Sandy. If we agree to give you a photo, will you leave us alone?' said Doug.

'Come on boys. I'll show you where to stand. OK, you, what's your name?'

'Doug.'

'Well, Doug, stand here and you...'

'Dave.'

'Ok, Dave, stand here,' said Sandy.

Other people also began to take photographs, as Sandy clicked away, moving them from one side to the other, covering different angles.

'Right, that will do,' said Doug.

'Let's go,' said Dave.

'No, no, wait,' shouted Sandy, as he followed them down the street. They weaved in and out of the crowd that was decreasing, trying to lose the Jock.

'Told you he wouldn't leave yer alone!' said Dave.

Doug looked behind as he turned the corner, 'No sign of him.'

'I seriously can't believe what we have just been through,' said Dave.

'I can't imagine what will happen in the next few days,' said Doug.

'Do you have any idea what that little Jock will put in the *Echo* tomorrow?' asked Dave.

'The mind boggles,' said Doug. 'Honestly, Hobbly, could yer actually believe what was happening? One minute, I was about to read the papers, then ferret in some boxes, now I won't ever know what was in them. Next we are looking at a wall of flames.'

'And, all because of a clumsy bastard,' said Dave. 'Yer know, they will make us out as heroes, Knowall. Yer only had to see how Sandy was laying it on.'

'Arsonists to heroes,' said Doug.

They walked past a public house, The Bird.

'Come on, let's have a pint, we deserve it,' suggested Dave. They sat down at a table near a window, sipping a pint of bitter.

'Tastes good,' said Doug.

'Just what was needed,' agreed Dave.

'I bet Vi's not happy with me,' said Doug.

'No, she'll get her own back, the next time she sees yer, she'll batter you round the ears with her enormous Bristols,' said Dave.

Just then they heard a familiar voice.

'Hello, boys, what are you having?' They looked over towards the bar and saw Sandy.

'Yer said you'd leave us alone,' said Dave.

'I need a story first. Two pints is it?' asked Sandy. 'Two pints of bitter, barman, and a double whisky,' said Sandy.

'The fire office said they won't let go, they're vultures,' said Dave.

'He was bloody right as well,' agreed Doug.

'Here you are, gentlemen, two of their best bitter,' said Sandy as he plonked himself down on a stool opposite them. 'Cheers.' He took a sip of his whiskey, then pulled out a notebook from his jacket pocket. They touched glasses. 'I have to say, from what I've heard, you two have been very brave, English bravery at its very best, and our leaders at the *Echo* are going to love you.'

Dave's look at Doug said it all, *What is this bloke all about, tosspot?*

'Got to put you in your best light. Two handsome young

men. Single… yes, single, now that's going to please our readers.

'Wait a minute, we're not looking to sign up for dates, with some *Echo* super girls or even grab a granny night out.'

'Well, you never know,' he looked at his notebook. 'David and Douglas.'

'No, Dave and Doug,' said Doug.

'And, how did yer get our names?' asked Dave.

'Addresses. Names and addresses, dear chaps, I need that information, don't I?' he said as he look a swig of whiskey.

'And how did yer know we were here?' asked Dave.

'Can't outfox the fox. Years of experience tells me if someone's trying to shake you off… try the nearest boozer.'

'What can we expect in yer rag tomorrow?' asked Doug.

'Rag, rag? The *Echo*'s no rag. Quality, young man, quality,' said Sandy.

'Yeah, OK, but what can we expect?' repeated Doug.

'You'll be front page, for sure, unless something major breaks to knock you off. Got some good photos for our team to work with, so we will do a good spread that you'll be proud of.'

Not at all sure about that, thought Dave.

'We'll get another drink, then get down the cop shop to see P.C. …Mellor,' said Dave.

'Yep, P.C. Mellor,' said Doug.

They left the pub after giving Sandy the story they wanted to tell, even though it was unlikely to be the *Echo*'s preference. They made a brief statement to P.C. Mellor, and were thanked and allowed to leave. On the way out they saw posters on a notice board; 'Beware of burglars', 'Beware of Thieves', 'Most

Wanted' and one that made them smile; 'Beware of Arsonists'.

'Where now?' asked Dave.

'Suppose I'd better nip back home, show me face, just in case Mum's heard anything.'

'Yeah OK, let's go,' replied Dave.

As Doug walked round the corner, he noticed a group of people outside his house.   'What's that lot doing?' said Doug.

'Dunno,' replied Dave. Getting closer they realised it was press. 'The vultures have landed on yer door step,' said Dave.

'Oh bollocks, surely we don't have to put up with this crap all the time,' said Doug as people rushed towards them.

'Mr Harris, Mr Thomas,' click, click, click. 'Can you give us a word, Mr Harris? Can you give us a few words Mr Thomas?' Click, click. They both pushed their way through.

'We've given a statement,' said Dave.

'Excuse me, excuse me,' said Doug, as he moved a cameraman to one side.

'Can you give us your side of the story?' asked a press man.

'We've given one,' said Doug.

Dave stopped, turning to face the press contingent, as Doug saw his ashen-faced mother open the front door.

'You'll all get the story, just give us a bit of peace,' said Dave as they both rushed through the door way, shutting the door firmly behind them.

'Are you in trouble?' asked Helen; she was visibly shaking.

'Calm down, Mum,' said Doug.

'Are you in trouble?' she repeated.

'No, not at all Mrs T., in fact the opposite, really,' said Dave.

'Yes, Mum. Local heroes,' said Doug, smiling. Helen began to make tea.

'Perhaps we can sit down and you two can tell me exactly what's happening, plus what are those people doing outside?' she said. They both sat down at the table, while Doug took a teaspoon and started tipping sugar to and fro in the sugar basin.

'We were on our way to Aunt Vi's this morning...'

Helen interrupted, 'I thought she'd have something to do with it, the trollop.'

'She hasn't, Mrs T.,' said Dave trying to suppress a laugh.

'No, Mum she hasn't anything to do with this,' said Doug.

'Thank God for that,' said Helen.

'As I was saying, Mum, we were walking down Essex Street this morning, when a fire broke out and we rescued a child,' said Doug.

'Fire, child?' said Helen.

'Yes, Mrs T., a fire, we rescued a little girl.'

'How's the child, is she OK?'

'Calm down, Mum. The child's all right,' said Doug.

Helen placed two cups of tea on the table. 'Stop playing with that sugar.'

'So that's why the press boys are parked outside,' said Dave. They all heard a rattling of the letter box.

'Who's that?' asked Helen.

'It's the press Mrs T., they won't go away,' said Dave.

'Let's sit down, Mum, work out a way to get rid of them.'

'How bad was the fire?' She asked, before sitting down.

'It was mainly the bedroom,' said Doug.

'And, was the child in that bedroom?'

'Yes, Mum.'

'How old is she?' asked Helen.

'About, six, seven months maybe, Mrs. T.'

'Oh, the poor soul. Are you sure she's OK?' said Helen.

'She's fine, Mrs T. They took her to hospital as a precaution, a precaution that's all,' said Dave.

'Now, what do we do about the vultures outside?' asked Doug.

'I suggest we let two in, give them the story, then kick 'em out,' said Dave.

'Sounds about right, as long as we are firm with 'em, it should be OK,' said Doug.

'Should I make tea for them?' asked Helen.

'No, don't want 'em moving in,' said Doug.

'I dunno, Knowall, perhaps a cuppa will go down well with those outside, after all, it's pretty cold,' said Dave.

'OK, I'll make it,' said Helen.

CHAPTER 11
E FIT

Detective Milne heard a knock on the door.

'Come in,' he shouted.

P.C. Wells and John, the security guard, entered a small office.

'Take a seat,' said Dennis, pointing to a chair on the other side of a desk. P.C. Wells was holding a large book, with an assortment of criminal photographs, known as mug shots. The young officer placed two small photos in front of Dennis, and said 'Although John couldn't recognise anyone from the album, these two show a similar likeness.'

'OK, officer, we'll take a look at them. I will bring the photos back when I'm done. Now, John, tell me why these two show a likeness.'

The door shut as P.C. Wells left the room.

'Bone structure, eyes and nose.'

Dennis put the photos to one side. 'Now, let's see if we can make up our own face.'

On the desk was a large box with pieces of cardboard, in

stacks, containing pictures of eyes, noses, chins, etc. And, taking pieces from each section, they gradually built up a face, until finally they were satisfied it resembled a likeness.

'That's good,' said John.

Taking the other two photos, Dennis compared them. 'Hmm, not bad. Are you happy with what we've produced or do you need to change anything?' asked Dennis.

'No, I think it's good.'

'When you first saw the intruder was anything unusual about his eyes? For example, did he have a squint, prominent stare or excessive blinking?' John shook his head. 'How about ears, ear lobes, eyebrows, his teeth – were they protruding, did they have gaps between any of the front ones, or even false?'

'Don't think so,' said John.

'Was he hunched in any way? Hands, tattoos, anything unusual about the fingers?'

John again shook his head from side to side.

'Now, what about his hair? Was it tinted? Have you considered the possibility of it being a wig?'

'I don't think it was a wig. Tinted, hmm, a possibility, maybe.'

'Finally, when you entered reception, picture him in front of you. Is there anything that stood out?'

'The glasses and the stain on his trousers, that's what really stood out.'

Dennis tapped a pen gently on his thumb, as he contemplated how things should proceed from now on in; should he place prominence on the leg or down grade its importance? He was edging towards it being the result of a fall; that was likely to heal quickly and so not be in the fore when it came to identification.

'Right, John. I think that will be all. We will get this photo printed and distributed. Thank you for coming in, you have my number, so if you recall anything that you regard as important, then give me a call. I'll show you out.'

They shook hands, then he picked up the photos from the table. Once he had showed John out, he went in search of P. C Wells.

'Here's your photo,' as he sat down next to the officer. 'Take a look at this,' he placed the made up photo on the table.

'It's a likeness to these two,' said P.C. Wells, adding, 'he seems a little confused about the hair, a bit hesitant in general.'

'I agree. I get this feeling he's not fully telling the truth, but I have no idea why,' said Milne. 'We'll go with what he's given us and hope it pays dividends. I'm definitely hopeful that come next week we will uncover a few answers.'

CHAPTER 12
CELEBRATING

'Thank you, Mr Thomas, for being straight with us,' said the reporter as they left the house and Doug closed the door behind them.

'Phew, glad that's done and dusted,' said Dave.

'I thought they were true gentlemen,' said Helen.

'Gentlemen, I don't think,' said Doug.

'Have yer got any beer in the fridge?' asked Dave.

'None,' replied Doug.

'I could murder one,' said Dave.

'Are yer going down The Crown later?' asked Doug.

'Dunno if I fancy it tonight,' replied Dave.

'It's Friday, can't stay in unless yer ill,' said Doug.

The telephone, rang.

'Hello, Helen speaking. Oh, hello Maurice. Yes, he's here. I'll pass you over.'

'Hiya, Oilrag. Well, what yer heard then...? Yeah, a fire. That's right Oily. Yes, we did rescue a child. Yer kidding. On the radio about half hour ago? I expect so; see yer down there tonight. Bye.'

'It's been on the radio,' said Doug.

'Where will it all end?' asked Dave.

'I'll get ready, what yer doing, Hobbly?'

'OK. I'll go home to get changed, call round when yer ready,' said Dave.

'Tell yer what. About 10 o'clock why don't we all go for a Chinese,' said Doug.

'Yeah, fancy a Chop Suey. Right, see yer later.'

Doug knocked on the door.

'It's open,' called Dave. Doug pushed open the door and entered.

'Pooh, what the hell's that?' asked Doug.

'Aftershave, Knowall.'

'Aftershave, what range is that, stinkbomb?'

'It will grow on yer,' said Dave.

'So will fertiliser, pooh,' replied Doug. 'Vi phoned after yer went.'

'What did she say?'

'Said I let her down, that she had a nice lunch waiting for me.'

'What was that, breast feed?' said Dave.

'Dumplings most likely,' said Doug.

'Better take a few bob out with us, shall we Knowall?'

'If we go for a Chinese meal. Yeah, shall we treat the lads?' asked Dave.

'If yer like, but don't go flashing it around, Hobbly.'

'It won't cost much, as long as they don't go over the top,' said Dave.

'Take a couple of quid for the meal, you and me, also a bit of small change. Shall we try the one in Crosby Street? Reckon it's supposed to be good,' said Doug.

'I don't mind. Me mum can't wait for the *Echo* tomorrow. I'm apprehensive.'

'Me too, the little Jock worries the life out of me,' said Dave.

'It's all a bit much. Now, this lot earlier, who's next?' said Doug. He passed some money to Dave.

'If yer ready let's go,' said Dave.

'What time do yer make it?' asked Doug.

'Bang on 7 o'clock.' They walked through the door of The Crown to a tumultuous applause. First to greet them were, not surprisingly, Lanky Pete, Tony, Bob and Maurice. 'All right lads, let them through,' shouted Len. 'Here you are, have two pints on the house,' as he shook them by the hand.

'Come here you two,' said Glenda, first giving Doug a kiss on a check, then the same to Dave. 'Cheers' rang out again. 'Jailhouse Rock' blared out on the jukebox, amusing Dave as it did so. 'Tell us, what happened?' asked Glenda.

'We've spoken too much, can yer read the local rag tomorrow, don't have to wait long,' said Doug.

'Is it right you saved a baby?' asked Len.

'Yeah, we did,' replied Doug. Another cheer, another slap on the back.

'They should get a medal for what they've done, Tony,' said Bob.

'You're right,' said Maurice.

'Spot on,' said Tony.

'It must have took some guts, don't think I could have done it,' said Pete.

'Me neither,' said Maurice. 'To put your life on the line like that is incredible.'

Dave was smiling as he heard Maurice, 'If yer only knew, it was a result of yer clumsy mate Knowall, none of this would be happening.' Fucking idiot, thought Dave.

'Get that drink down you, let me buy you another one. Two pints Len,' said Paddy Byrne.

'Two coming up, Paddy.'

'What do you think of them, Glenda?' asked Brenda, one of the regulars.

'Proud of them. Amazing courage,' replied Glenda.

'Thanks everyone,' shouted Doug.

'I'll second that,' said Dave.

'Can we go through to the other bar?' asked Doug, among even louder cheers.

'Make way, make way,' said Lanky Pete. They were soon sat in their regular seats as more regulars came in to shake both their hands.

'Drink up, let's get you two another one,' said Tony.

'Yer trying to get us drunk,' said Dave.

'Be pissed by 10 o'clock at this rate,' said Doug.

'Talking about 10 o'clock. We're thinking of going for a Chinese later, do yer all fancy it, lads?' said Dave.

'Have a bit of that,' said Pete.

'Get the prawn balls down you, Monkey,' said Tony.

'Orange had duck last time, he's been quackers ever since,' replied Bob. Laughter rang out.

'What do you normally have, Maurice?' asked Pete.

'Sweet and sour, can't beat it. Sweet and sour chicken, with loads of beansprouts.'

'Yer making me feel hungry,' said Dave.

'What about you, Pete?' asked Tony.

'He looks at the menu for an hour before he decides,' said Doug.

'Tell you what I'll have now,' they all waited in anticipation. 'Number 22 with rice and prawn balls.' Again laughter broke out.

'Nelly wants to see you two heroes in the saloon bar,' said Glenda.

'Oh God,' said Dave. 'Alright Glenda, tell her we'll be through shortly.'

'Have to get used to it,' said Bob.

'You'll be on telly next,' said Pete.

'Shut up,' said Dave.

'Be on the early evening show. What's it called?' asked Maurice.

'Is it called, "Our Region"?' said Tony.

'No, it's called, "In Town",' said Bob.

'Come on, Hobbly, better not keep Nelly waiting,' said Doug. They walked through to the saloon bar, amid more back clapping. Clapping broke out as soon as they appeared through the doorway.

'What have you boys been up to? Let me get you a drink,' said Nelly.

'No, we'll get you one. Give us a stout Glenda, please. What about yer, Mavis. Make it two stouts please, Glenda.'

'So, tell us what's happened, Douglas, your mum must be so proud of you,' said Nelly.

'Yes, she is. We just rescued a child from a fire,' said Doug.

'Make it sound so easy,' said Mavis.

'Well I suppose it was, really, no big deal,' said Dave as he put two stouts on the table.

'Well, we think you're both very brave, very brave indeed,' replied Nelly.

'We agree,' said other drinkers.

'Well, thank you all,' said Doug.

'What did Helen say about it?' asked Mavis.

'She's still in shock, Mavis,' replied Doug.

'Is the child alright, David?' asked Nelly.

'She's OK, took her off to hospital as a precaution.'

'Poor soul,' said Mavis. 'Here's two pints from Tony said Glenda,' and she put them on the counter.

'Two whiskeys for you. I'll leave them next to your pints,' said Len.

'Who they from?' asked Doug.

'Oh, from Eric.'

'Cheers, Eric,' said Doug.

'OK, I'll tell him,' said Len.

'Can't drink whiskey, better give 'em to the ladies,' said Dave.

'Would yer like a whiskey, ladies?' said Doug.

'Love one, bit of water with it, please, Douglas.'

'Me too,' said Mavis.

'Will it be in the papers?' asked Nelly.

'Local rag tomorrow,' said Doug.

'Make sure we get one tomorrow,' said Mavis.

'You both need to see Father Rowley to give thanks,' said Nelly.

'Oh yes, you must,' said Mavis.

'I'm sure we will sometime,' said Doug, smiling at Glenda, who realised there was next to no chance of doing it. 'Here's a jug of water ladies,' said Doug placing it on the table.

'Thank you ladies and gentleman, must be going,' said Dave.

'We will see yer again, Nelly, Mavis,' said Doug.

'Goodbye, boys,' said Nelly as they disappeared from the saloon bar. 'Lovely boys,' said Nelly.

'Thanks for the whiskey, Eric,' said Dave.

'Yeah, cheers Eric,' said Doug.

They could hear laughter coming from the other side of the door. 'The lads are in good form tonight,' said Doug as they walked through and took their regular seats.

'Go on, tell them,' said Pete.

'Listen to this one,' said Bob.

'Go on Tony,' repeated Pete.

'OK. I went out with my brother-in-law on Wednesday night. I'm skint.'

'Nothing new there then,' said Doug.

'Anyway, the beers are on him, plus he bungs me a few bob, loaded he is. We started at The Plough, the beers going down well, so we move on to The Star. Then it's The Bugle followed by The Butchers. It's now about 9.30. I'm also about three quarters pissed. I vaguely remember talking to some bird, but sod all else, until I wake up next morning. I opened my eyes no idea where I am, and hear someone breathing like a horse.'

'Nay, nay you didn't,' said Bob.

'She didn't look much better either,' said Tony. 'I shot out of bed. I don't remember a thing about last night. What have I done? Are you lot playing a joke on me or what? It's 5.30, never been up so early in my life. For the next half hour I pace up and down the kitchen trying to recall anything from the previous night, but nothing, a complete mystery, I look in on her, she's now snoring, well away, I shook my head in disbelief. Do you know what, strange really, I vaguely remember, only vaguely mind, lying on this bird and thinking, for Christ's sake, make a bleedin' effort woman, but I thought it was a dream.'

'Perhaps you were riding a horse at Ascot,' said Pete.

'Yeah, like the ones I back, they certainly don't put in much effort,' said Maurice. Everyone laughed and banged tables.

'I'm now in a right state. I need to get to the bottom of this. So, I start making a noise, banging a few cupboards, stamping my feet, drilling a few holes in the wall, anything to wake her up and get her out of there. I must have woken up half the street, but still she's in dreamland, unbelievable. She eventually surfaced at 10 o'clock, then joined me in the kitchen wearing only bra and panties. I don't see her getting a modelling contract in the near future. All I can think is, I haven't, have I? For a moment, I panicked further; I haven't asked her to move in, surely not. She came over, threw her arms round me and gave me a bear hug, life drained out of me for a moment or two. "Shall we have breakfast, then go back to bed?" she laughed just like an outboard motor. How do I get out of this? She started pecking at my neck. Will you stop it for Christ's sake, I thought. Suddenly I found my voice. "Work. Got to go to work," I said. "Work? You said you had a day off," she replied. "No, should have been there two hours ago." "This is very disappointing. Perhaps you can make it up to me, tonight," she said pinching me on the bottom. "Tonight, tonight, can't make it tonight. Look I need to go. Leave your contact number, then I'll call you sometime. Can you let yourself out?" I asked. "Yes, call me," she said. "Ok, bye." With that I was gone.

'That's what drink does for you, numbs the head,' said Bob.

'Can't numb his brain, he don't have one,' said Doug.

'I haven't been drunk since,' said Tony.

'It's less than 48 hours ago, you idiot,' said Pete.

'Oh yeah,' said Tony. 'I know one thing, I won't be repeating that again, complete mystery, not putting myself through that, frightening.'

'We've all had nights similar to that, I expect women get the same experience, going to bed with some God's gift to women, then once the beer wears off, waking up next to a washed up, short-sighted, pill-popping, weakling, wearing pink underpants. She will likely conclude, a tin of pineapple chunks more enjoyable than he,' said Dave.

'I'm starving,' said Doug.

'Well, the last place you want is a Chinese restaurant,

because you eat it, then half hour later, you're starving again,' said Bob.

'Right, it's 9.20, shall we go for a Chinese, what do yer think lads? Those for… four. Against… two. Cooky rooky it is then,' said Dave. Glenda, is Len about?'

'I'll get him.'

Len came round, 'What is it, Dave?'

'We're going for a Chinese meal.'

'Who's we?'

'Just the lads, Len,' whispered Dave out of earshot of the others.

'If it's not too late, you're sober and you want a lock in, knock the window in the saloon bar,' said Len.

'Alright, cheers Len. Let's drink up lads,' said Dave.

As they walked through the door way, single file, Len rang a bell. 'It's not last orders yet, but Dave and Doug are going, before they leave they would like to say a word or two.'

'Yer right, Len. Dear Friends, thank yer for a lovely evening,' said Dave. 'Cheers!'

'Like Dave, I thank yer all for a great evening and thank Glenda, Len.' They all left the pub and even outside they heard the loud applause and cheering.

It was decided on the new restaurant in Crosby Street. From the outside it looked promising.

'Table for six.'

'Follow me.'

They all admired the excellent decor, very impressive for a first time visit. Maurice looked at the menu, 'I think they have a lot more choice than the other place,' he said.

'We will have finished eating ours by the time Pete's ordered his,' said Tony.

'Could be right,' said Pete as he studied the menu.

'Hello boys, how the devil are you?'

'I don't believe it, Malcolm Lynch,' said Doug. The first and only black kid in our school when we were there from 1951–1966. Malcolm went round shaking each and everyone by the hand.

'Long time no see, Malc, what yer doing here?' asked Dave.

'I'm with my missus and family. Introduce you later.'

'How yer doing, Malc?' asked Pete.

'Good, man, good,' he replied.

'You look very smart in your whistle and flute,' said Tony.

'You look as though you're doing well for yourself,' said Maurice.

'I'm in business wid me dad.'

'Doing what exactly?' asked Dave.

'Undertaker. And no quips about black berrying,' replied Malcolm, with a broad smile.

'Jesus, you don't mean to say, you bury dead people,' said Pete.

'We don't bury them alive, man, wouldn't be much good for our business.'   Among the laughter you could hear Tony say, 'You pillock, Pete.'

He's always had a good sense of humour our Malcolm; he certainly needed it with our lot, thought Doug.

'Talk with you later, looks like my meal has arrived,' said

Malcolm.

'Well, what a surprise that was,' said Doug.

'Have we all got a drink?' asked Dave.

'Yes,' came the reply.

'Well I would like to make a toast to Maurice. Here's to Maurice,' they all raised a glass. 'I just realised earlier that it was three years ago today, Maurice. Do yer remember, Maurice?'

'Do I, do I? It was the day of my trial. Remember it well,' said Pete.

'Just like yesterday,' said Bob.

'It's amazing that it's three years today,' said Tony. 'I've never said this before, but I so much appreciated your support, lads. The experience was quite amazing.'

CHAPTER 13
THE TRIAL

Maurice's full name is Maurice Cecil Ford. Known as 'Oilrag'. Twenty-seven years old. Single. Car Mechanic. He's always had a fascination with cars, in particular the inner workings of engines. He could dismantle a car engine, then rebuild it, by the time he was nine years old. He did a three year apprenticeship with his uncle Eric when he left school. After years of hard graft he was now the proud owner of a successful small garage, training his own young apprentice.

All this was put on hold however, because of a few moments of madness, three years ago. Wendy Hick was a single parent, with a six-year-old daughter. She had just received the keys to a council flat, with no way of furnishing it. Maurice was a good friend of her brother, Vic. The more he spoke to Vic about her plight, the sorrier he felt for her. Secondhand would have been the answer. But, her knight in shining armour, Maurice the prat, knew different.

'We'll go down to Wheelers and help ourselves.' So, with the help of Vic, they did just that.

Maurice soon got a tug and was carted off down the nick. He refused to name Vic, telling the police he had worked alone. Not surprisingly they didn't believe him, how was he to manoeuvre heavy furniture round the warehouse, then onto a lorry, all on his lonesome. 'Tell yer what sunshine, join the next Olympic squad in the weight lifting category, bring a gold home.'

He was named 'Cecil' after his grandfather. He hoped this was not an omen, as his grandfather had spent time in prison. He'd been working at the town hall and was found guilty of fiddling the books to fund his extravagant lifestyle and womanising. Now, they say a sailor has a woman in every port. Cecil had a woman in every office, the dirty old git.

Maurice's only excuse, he said, was the fact that he'd made no gain, personally. So his mates were in court to give him support, and that was important to him. He was told that not naming Vic would go against him. So, I'll let you in on how we saw the case and the outcome.

We were walking along the road singing, 'There's only one Oilrag, one Oilrag, there's only one Oilrag.' Anyone would have thought we were on a boys outing to Brighton.

'Just look at Monkey, Wilson.' The prat was dressed in a bright yellow shirt and orange trousers, he looked like an ice cream and all he needed now was a beach ball, dark sunglasses and a pair of Jesus sandals. But, instead we – me Dave, Doug, Bob, Tony and Pete – were going to cheer on our mate, Oilrag, Maurice Ford, in his hour of need – in court.

On entering the court building yer could smell the strong

whiff of disinfectant. We got in to the court early, just to make sure of a good seat. Monkey insisted on arriving early; God only knows what he thought he was about to witness – strip show, most likely. We sat waiting for the big event to start, whilst looking at the decor, or lack of it. First impression, drab, certainly in need of freshening up. I'm thinking, when the magistrate man comes in, I can slip him a quote. Our little mob could do a good job, no problem, on the cheap, just as long as he didn't tell the dole office. Only trouble was the ceilings, bloody high, but that's where Lanky Pete comes into his own.

'Dunno why they can't play a bit of music while we wait,' Monkey asked me, 'do they dim the lights?'

Maurice was sitting in the bowels of the court, waiting to face the magistrate again. It was Judgement Day for thieving a cooker, fridge, T.V., bed, wardrobe, settee and radiogram. Incidentally, the radiogram never worked from day one, so he hoped that would be taken into account.

Not exactly the crime of the century, resulting in worldwide attention. A crime, yes, but the way he saw it he was in for a bollocking, slap on the wrist, kick up the arse, then out of there. Sooner the fucking better as far as he was concerned. No big deal. He was guilty and couldn't give a toss. But he didn't feel guilty. Well, about as guilty as a vicar caught humping one of his parishioners, he supposed.

The only regret, apart from getting caught, was hiring his solicitor, Mr Broadbent. Oh God, did I drop a bollock! Broad he wasn't. A right tosspot, reckoned Maurice. He was from a large respectable firm of lawyers. Don't know where they got him from exactly, under a stone maybe. Now he didn't expect the top man, no, not at all. Little further down the line was fair enough. But, not rock bottom. He must have been 101 in the pecking order, or else he was a cleaner moonlighting as a bogus lawyer. He was about 5'7" tall, spitting image of Mr Magoo the cartoon character, bald as a coot. He also had a dodgy right eye, that seemed to look round corners, because when he was looking directly at you, his right eye would be looking over your shoulder. Many a time Maurice looked around, expecting someone to be stood behind. A bit off-putting really. Made it hard to concentrate on what he was saying. Not as though he said much. Fuck only knows how he could justify charging for his services, or lack of it. He did nothing nor said anything worthwhile. Maurice reckoned he'd have been better off defending himself; at least he'd have got his name right. At one time he kept calling him Mick, the idiot.

'OK, Mr Ford, the court is ready for you,' said Mr Magoo.

A whisper swept through the court that proceedings were about to begin. Monkey expected the organ and player to rise out of the ground. The usher called for quiet, followed by 'All stand' as the magistrate entered. Oh dear, he looked very stern and quite miserable in fact, but then if you looked at anyone in the court, they weren't smiling. All right, so it's a serious business in most cases, but not all. Magistrates or crown court, liven it up a bit. Stick a juggler in the corner. Put a tightrope and walker above the judge's head. When the magistrate passes his sentence on a shoplifter, dress the magistrate up as a clown, with makeup and red nose, then stick a laughing sailor next to him.

Then Oilrag was called to the dock. *Sooner him than me,* I thought. I just didn't rate the bloke on the bench. We were giving it the thumbs up and trying to make him feel at ease. We were soon told to be quiet by Mr Bossman. Cheeky bastard, it's not like we were chanting 'there's only one Oilrag', all we were doing was wishing him well; he was gonna need it.

Maurice was stood in the dock again, his trial nearing an end, carried over from yesterday. He looked towards his mates; they were thumbing it and all sorts, and then were told to shut up. No change in the magistrate today, still miserable. Maurice was convinced he was on a downer, because he'd just been turned down as 'grumpy' in this year's panto. Yesterday had gone OK; no real problems and an ex-employer had given him a good character reference. The lads wanted to speak up for him, but he said he'd take his chances, rather than they get him hung, drawn and quartered.

Then it turned against him. He was stood down and Mr Wheeler, who owns the shop from where Maurice helped himself, took the stand. He said, 'I haven't worked extremely hard 24/7 for years to build up a successful business, just for some thieving yob to come along and steal it.' Maurice admits he even had a certain amount of sympathy for him. For a moment he thought, you rotten thieving bastard, until he realised it was him he was talking about.

He certainly sealed Maurice's fate. If you listened to Mr Wheeler you'd have thought he'd just nicked the crown jewels or even pinched the Queen's arse. Still it went on and on and on, until the main man adjourned for lunch.

Maurice needed a break after listening to that; couldn't get much worse, he thought. Wrong.

He was sitting in a little room with 'Magoo' sat opposite, with just a table in between.

'You'll be found guilty,' said Magoo, oddly smiling when he said it.

Well, nothing fucking new there then. I've already held me hands up to it, you doughnut, Maurice thought.

'I'm looking forward to this,' Magoo said as he took the lid off his lunchbox. 'Would you like one?' he asked, offering Maurice a sandwich, which he declined. Mind you, that's if you could call them sandwiches; one bite and they would have been devoured, if it had been Maurice. Cut in little triangles, no crust, exactly the same they were, as if they'd been measured. It was almost a shame to eat them, might have been better off in some sort of catering exhibition. His old dear must have been up since the crack of dawn, cutting them up. He'd have been better off with a packet of crisps and a pickled egg. 'Cheese again,' he said, shaking his head slightly and giving out a sigh. 'I told her, ham. Fed up with cheese, day in, day out, and it's cheese. I think we need a change, now and again, don't you?' he said looking at Maurice. Well, he thought he was anyway. 'I'm not a mouse, for goodness' sake,' he said. *About as useful,* Maurice thought. Maurice thought he was going to start crying, the dozy pillock: 'Yer should have seen his face, you'd have thought he had just pulled a bird, only to realise it was a bloke. Mind you, he'd have probably settled for that.'

'Said to her this morning,' Magoo continued, '"Joan dear,

do you think I could have ham, today?" "Yes, dear," she replied. Always calls me dear, never Dennis, always dear. "And, pickle," I said, love my pickle, I do. Oh, dear,' he said shaking his head, again. 'You know what. She hasn't even put pickle on them.' It was getting too much for him but still he went on, 'I really must have a word with her tonight. It's just not good enough, is it?' He looked at Maurice, who nodded. Buggered if he knew why, but he just nodded. 'Dear, dear, dear, I don't know, must have a word, tonight,' he said, as he took a nibble out of a sandwich.

Talk about priorities. Now, here I am about to get sentenced and Magoo's worried about a poxy sandwich. I mean who gives a toss whether it's ham or cheese. And, who gives a toss whether she calls him 'dear' or 'Dennis'. I'm buggered if I do, thought Maurice.

'You'll be all right,' said Magoo.

Here he goes again, Maurice thought. *If he's told me once, he's told me a thousand times that I'll be all right. I'm sure he's trying to convince himself, not me.* Now he was fearing the worst, nothing was going to his liking and he got the impression that Magoo was in the wrong profession, he wasn't cut out to be a lawyer; bingo caller maybe. Now he was relying on his wisdom. *God help me, I'd have settled for Norman Wisdom,* thought Maurice.

Magoo then excels himself and comes out with a classic, the imbecile. 'You just apologise to the magistrate; well, grovel a bit.'

'Grovel,' Maurice said.

'Yes, grovel a bit, just a bit,' he replied.

'How the hell can I grovel in front of my mates? It's not right, it's like having a bath with your socks on, not right.' *I'm in the shit, so let's get it over, before I strangle Magoo,* thought Maurice.

'Phew, that Wheeler chap laid it on a bit. Over the top if yer ask me. Definitely looks like boss-man has it in for Oily, urging Wheeler to give a damning account. Get the trowel out man and lay it on thick, shed a few tears, rip a few clothes, even stick yer missus and kids on the front row looking like starving refugees. Poor Oilrag.'

'Will you stop it, Monkey. I said earlier, the ushers are not here to sell ice cream.'

'These ushers must walk miles during cases, great way to lose weight. I've just seen an elderly woman usher give the magistrate a piece of paper to read, it looks as if she's been overdoing it, she looks so thin, seen more fat on a chip.'

The bossman did the only good thing he's done so far when he adjourned for lunch. We needed it after listening to the Wheeler chap's hatchet job. We all gathered outside the court in a newly designed garden, with rows of flower beds and wooden benches. Somewhere really peaceful for defendants to contemplate their fate, before some humourless magistrate bangs them up in a poky cell for the next three months. We were all giving our pennies' worth, for what good that was, on Oilrag's fate. The general consensus was not favourable, as we gave our predictions. Tony thought two months' jail. Doug thought three months' jail. Pete thought the stuff was planted on him, fit up, and should be released. How exactly you plant a cooker, fridge, T.V., bed, wardrobe, settee and radiogram, even though it didn't work, on some unsuspecting bloke, without him knowing… Pete couldn't answer. Maurice thought four months' jail, but desperately wanted to be wrong and Monkey didn't know, but thought the catering should be better. The wait should be over soon.

'The end is nigh, end is nigh,' said Magoo. Maurice didn't know why he'd spoken these words, the only conclusion he could come to was the man was a complete prat. 'Court One is ready for you. Well, my friend we have done our best for you,' said Magoo. Here comes that silly smile.

I'd question whether he's done his best for me. If that had been the case, he'd have emigrated long ago, thought Maurice. *And I'm certainly not his friend and never will be.*

'Don't forget to throw yourself on the mercy of the court. Grovel, man, grovel well,' said Magoo as they ascended the stairs to court.

You're so close to being strangled, you bald headed moron, thought Maurice.

They entered the court, which was quite packed. Maurice looked over to see his mates, giving them the thumbs up, just maybe for the last time in a while. He sat twiddling his thumbs and fingers, waiting for Mr Misery to do his duty. He was at peace with himself, calm, ready to accept the decision, good or bad, freedom or jail, do the time, then get on with life.

'All stand.' He stood up; his legs felt like jelly, he didn't expect that.

'Remain standing, Mr Ford,' said the magistrate, as he took his seat.

Don't put on the black hat, Maurice thought, smiling to himself.

'Do you wish to say anything in your defence?' the magistrate asked.

'No Sir,' Maurice replied, looking over at Magoo. When Maurice said it, Magoo's face reddened, showing a little anger at his reply with daggers aimed in his direction. There was a short pause and Maurice missed the magistrate's first few words. He was deep in thought but then clearly heard the following words, 'You have behaved appallingly. I must protect people from the likes of you. Have you shown remorse? Not one morsel. You helped yourself, as if it were your right. I have no hesitation in giving you a custodial sentence. You will be sent to prison for three months. Take him away.'

Maurice was led away a little numb after hearing he was off to jail and even though he did think it likely, it was still a shock. *But after all is said and done, I bloody deserve it,* Maurice thought.

We felt shock and sadness that we had witnessed our mate being sent down. All right, we thought it might happen, but by God, it still came as a shock, big shock. We all left court, with none of us able to speak, it was just surreal.

Three months. That's twelve weekends. That's Friday night, Saturday night and Sunday night, staying in… seems a lifetime. No pub, club or nooky. Wow. Soon as he got out it would be

London West End for him.

We waited an hour at the back of the court to see a paddy wagon appear with Oilrag, before it drove off to prison. We gave him a cheer just to let him know we were still around. Bob and Pete would visit him at the earliest possible date. The outcome wasn't to our liking, but it was a good experience to see how the law functioned and was administered. We all thought the magistrate wasn't impartial, favouring Mr Wheeler. We would make sure Oilrag's garage was safe from any thieving toe rag breaking in. He'd be out soon, just in time for Christmas; that would make us all merry. There's only one Oilrag, bless him.

CHAPTER 14
WHAT'S IN THE ECHO

'Wake up. Wake up.'

'Wait a minute, wait,' shouted Dave as he let Doug into his bedsit. 'Me head,' he said, as he rubbed his forehead. 'What time is it?'

'Quarter to ten.'

Dave noticed he was in clothes from the previous night. 'What day is it?'

'Saturday, yer were a bit worse for wear, we had to carry yer home and dump yer on the bed,' said Doug.

'We had a session in The Crown, didn't we?' said Dave.

'Didn't we. A late one,' said Doug. 'Have a look at the rag.'

'LOCAL HEROES' was the headline in the *Echo* newspaper, with a picture of both looking up at the burnt-out window.

'Big Splash,' said Dave, 'tell me the gist.'

'Well, yer have the front cover, four pages inside with dramatic pictures of the fire, followed by a load of bullshite.

Little Jock fella excelled himself, with truth being substituted by his take on things; that's what we expected.'

'Moron's in the wrong profession, should have been a politician, few of them could lay straight in bed,' said Dave.

'Apparently yer went back into the fire three times to rescue the kid. I held back falling debris so yer could crawl through a gap, with the kid. We just made it out in time, another ten seconds and we would have been burnt alive and finally, we were almost electrocuted. No wonder we are heroes,' said Doug.

'How are people going to react after reading that garbage,' said Dave.

'Makes yer wanna tell the truth,' said Doug.

'Dare not do that, we'd get lynched,' said Dave.

'Just have to go along with it, got no other choice,' said Doug.

'Tell yer what, Knowall, I'm bloody glad my mum and dad are living in Australia. What's yer mum going to make of it?' said Dave.

'I think she believed it all, every word. She went to get the papers early, must have read it three or four times. I left her with Barbara chewing over the story. I walked from my place to here; I should imagine at least ten people have congratulated me, didn't know them from Adam, weird. How do these people that are always in the spotlight cope with all this crap? Soon jack it in, wouldn't yer, Hobbly?'

'Sad to say really, but we have to use this to our advantage,' said Doug.

'I feel a bit of a fraud. And, sadly, I suppose yer right, Knowall.'

'Who knows, may get in nightclubs free, with the lads of course, given special treatment, get all the birds throwing themselves at us, might not be all bad,' said Doug.

'I'm fed up with it already,' said Dave.

'Another thing that will piss yer off a bit, the mighty *Echo* says give 'em a medal.'

'Yer what?' said Dave. 'Give 'em a medal? Oh, please.'

'It's true, that's what it said, Hobbly.'

'What do yer want to do about the money, Knowall?'

'What do yer mean?'

'Do yer want to divide it up and take it home?'

'Maybe we can sort it out next week, but not now,' said Doug.

'What's on the cards today then, Knowall?'

'Dunno. Normally it's down the pub for lunchtime drink, alas this ain't normal, Hobbly.'

'Give it a month, we will be opening special events, opening new hospitals, kissing babies and having a night out with Prince Charles. Where will it all end?' said Dave. 'First thing to do is pick out a yankee bet, my regular donation to the book maker.'

'Yer know I can't remember the last time I had a touch,' said Doug.

'I was told a horse for Newbury and it's gone out of my head,' said Dave.

'Who gave yer that tip?' asked Doug.

'Creeping Jesus.'

'He's a crap tipster.'

'No, he's given me a few crackers. 100/8 winner 10/1 he's not bad. Do yer remember that time in the tavern when we were having a pint? Tony was reading the paper and the table kept wobbling. It really started to annoy him. In comes Creeping Jesus giving it some rabbit. Tony said you're supposed to be a carpenter, fix this fucking table. Creeping really copped the needle. I'll have to look for that horse at Newbury, he reckoned it had a chance,' said Dave.

'What's the name?' asked Doug, 'think.'

'Something to do with religion, I think. Is it, The sabbath, The Cross, Christianity. No, none of them rings a bell. Better look in the paper,' said Dave.

'What about Good Friday?'

'That's it, that's what it was called.'

'What, Good Friday?' asked Doug.

'No… Hot Cross Buns,' replied Dave.

'Morning love, cold again outside. You're out early this morning my sweet,' said Charles.

'Run out of milk, so I nipped out to get some and the morning paper,' said Grace the adoring wife of Charles. 'Relax today, love; take your mind off work for a change. I'm making tea, so what would you like for breakfast?'

'Couple of boiled eggs and toast would be nice, my love.'

'Have a look at the paper, it's all about that fire, horrendous,' said Grace.

Charles sat down at the kitchen table then put the paper in front of him. 'Oh my word, that's incredible.'

'Can't believe those two young men went into that house to

save a baby, just amazing,' said Grace.

Charles turned over the page to reveal more graphic photos. 'Look at that fire. It's remarkable that they could accomplish what they did, without any training. I take my hat off to them,' said Charles.

'They look so young,' said Grace.

'The chief will see you now.' The secretary opened the door to a large office and introduced firemen James Butler and Les Cork.

'Sit down gentlemen,' said Chief Fire Officer, Roger Lee. 'Have you seen today's *Echo* newspaper?'

'Yes sir,' they both replied.

'Good. I've called you in here as a matter of urgency. Let me explain. We have just two weeks before our very important fire prevention week. My aim is to get these two,' pointing to the front of the paper, 'to head our poster campaign. I would like us to hold a reception and a special award in recognition of outstanding bravery. I want you, Les, as communications officer, to work alongside James to make this happen.'

'Yes, sir.'

'Twenty-four hours ago these two were unknown, they will soon be household names when people see the pictures and hear of the bravery shown; it will energise all. We need to tap into this immediately, hence the urgency I'm giving it, James.'

'I agree, sir.'

'Les.'

'Yes sir, agree.'

'I don't want any of this made public, until all the i's are dotted and t's are crossed. Leave it to me to try and persuade Douglas and David. Make me an appointment with them for next Friday morning, at this station, if possible. The clock is ticking gentlemen. Any questions?'

'No sir,' came the reply.

'P.C. Wells, P.C. Marsh. P.C. Walker. I've made you all aware of the Whites Engineering case,' said detective Milne. 'I've selected you three to carry out important investigations relating to that crime. P.C. Walker. Do you know Craven Road? Do you know it well?'

'I know of it, but not well.'

'Familiarise yourself with it, especially the end by the fence overlooking Whites,' said Milne.

'Yes, sir,' said Walker.

'You'll be given a photo of our suspect sometime today. From tomorrow, Tuesday, through to and including Friday between 8am and 9.30, your job will be to stop anyone going to and fro, then ask if they recognise the photo or if they saw anything suspicious the previous Thursday between 8.15am and 9.15. Anyone loitering sat in a car, anything out of the ordinary. Is that clear?' asked Milne.

'Yes, sir,' replied Walker.

'P.C. Wells, P.C. Marsh. We've just been given permission to erect a poster tomorrow outside White's Engineering, on the grass verge. On this poster will be a blown up photo of our suspect. You know the sort of thing, have you seen this man, etcetera. On Thursday morning only, between 8am and 9.30, you will stop traffic outside White's and ask the same questions relating to seven days previous and around the same time. Any questions?'

'How long will the poster stay?' asked Wells.

'About a week,' replied Milne. 'Anything else?'

'No, sir,' came the replies.

'Ok, I'll find out about the photos,' said Milne. Just then the telephone rang, 'Morning Milne, speaking. Yes… that's right… good. Yes, Tuesday. Fine… Thank you for calling. Good news. Photos will be here at 2 o'clock and the poster will be up by 4pm this afternoon. Thanks gentlemen, I will catch up with you later.'

'OK, Aunt Vi, I promise I won't leave it so long next time,' said Doug.

'Goodbye sweetie.'

'Bye Vi,' said Dave.

'Christ. 5.30. Didn't realise we were in there that long,' said Doug.

'What a case she is and some knockers,' said Dave.

'Well blessed,' said Doug.

'I want to go to The Crown to see Len. And then I'm having a quiet night after the mayhem of the last four, five days,' said Dave.

'We've had a hectic time, ain't we, how did we fit it all in?' said Doug.

'Here, you're the one's in the paper,' said a passer-by.

'It is them,' said a woman. 'Good on yer mate, let me shake

you by the hand,' he put out his hand, which they accepted. 'Well done, fellas,' said the woman. A couple more people stopped to do the same before they reached the pub.

'Evening Len, a couple of pints please,' said Doug.

'How are you boys?' said Len.

'A little quieter tonight,' said Dave.

'By the way, two fellas were in lunchtime looking for you,' said Len.

'Any idea who?' asked Doug.

'No wouldn't say, but will be back later, is all they said.'

'Well, well here they are now,' said Len as they saw two men approaching.

'Will you allow me to get those drinks?' asked Les. 'I'll have a pint of bitter and you, James?'

'An orange juice please, landlord.'

'Let me introduce ourselves. Les Cork, and he is James Butler, we represent the fire service.'

'Oh, pleased to meet anyone from the service,' said Doug.

'What can we do for yer?' asked Dave.

'Is there anywhere we can talk in private?' asked Les.

'Could go through to the saloon bar, should be quiet this time of night.'

Les paid for the drinks, then followed them through. Once they were settled the conversation began.

'Our fire chief, Roger Lee would like to meet with you both to discuss some business. I'm sorry that I can't discuss details at the moment,' said Les.

'Secret is it,' said Doug.

'Not secret, just hush-hush for the time being,' said James.

After a little banter, they finally agreed to meet with Roger Lee on Friday at 10am despite still being in the dark. 'Do yer two want a game of bar billiards?' asked Dave.

'Don't mind, we got time,' said James.

'Right, eads or tails?' asked Dave.

'Heads,' called James.

'Heads it is,' said Doug.

'We'll take the break,' said Les.

'I think I'll let you break off, James.'

He started well and continued until he broke down. '16,370 break over. He's played before, the bandit,' said Dave.

'Be back in a mo, just gonna see Len, then I'm in for an early.'

'How are you coping with this new found fame?' asked Les.

'Some of it's good, some not so,' said Doug.

'Not sure Dave's liking it much,' said James.

'He's struggled with it from day one, to be honest. Bit of advice, he's stubborn, very stubborn,' said Doug, smiling.

'Bye, David.'

'Bye, Mrs. T.'

'We'll be back later to let yer know, Mum.'

'Make sure you do,' said Helen, as she shut the front door behind them.

'Should take about twenty minutes to get there, shouldn't it?' said Dave.

'About that. Wonder what's behind it?' asked Doug.

'Perhaps they'll fast track yer to fireman, Douglas.' I'm no good to 'em, they don't want a Hobbly,' said Dave.

'Might take yer on, just to ring the bell on shouts, ding, ding. At least this is something different, it's all been so manic of late,' said Doug.

'I got a takeaway last night, wouldn't let me pay for it,' said Dave.

They soon reached the station. They'll be impressed with this – look, 9.58,' said Dave.

'Morning,' said James as he escorted them up to a conference room where they were welcomed by chief Roger Lee and Les. After a firm handshake from Roger, they were asked to take a seat.

'Anything to drink?' asked Les.

'I'll have a white coffee,' said Dave.

'Same for me, thanks,' said Doug.

Les and James served the coffee before taking a seat. 'Right gentlemen, thank you for coming. You know Les and you've met James.'

'The bandit,' said Dave.

'A county player at bar billiards, I understand,' said a smiling Roger. 'I suspect you're wondering why I've asked you here today. Well, its twofold. One, we wish to hold a reception next Friday at the town hall, to honour you both with a special award for outstanding bravery.'

'Not sure that's a good idea,' said Dave.

'And you, Douglas?'

'Well, call me Doug for a start. I'm not sure.'

'Well, we need to discuss it. Two, we have a fire prevention week coming up soon, a week's time in fact. Prevention week saves so many lives and our poster campaign for prevention week is the most important that we undertake in any given year. We would love you to come on board and head our campaign.'

'Wow,' said Doug, while Dave sat stoney-faced.

Roger took a quick glance at Les. 'Can I say, because of your bravery it has propelled you to the top. Your actions and words alone will save lives,' said Les.

'Yes, I agree, profoundly. I don't think you quite realise just what impact you could make,' said Roger.

'Just think, if your taking part saved one life it would be worth it,' said James.

'How would we take part in this?' asked Dave.

'Yes, what exactly would we be doing?' said Doug.

A slight relief came over Les. 'You two would be the main faces on our poster campaign, you will be photographed professionally. This will be unveiled next Friday,' said Roger.

'We are on a tight timescale,' said Les.

'Yes, on Monday you will need to meet with accounts, legal teams to discuss payment and sign contracts. Can I leave this with you, Les?' Les nodded. 'What do you think gentleman?'

'Ok with me,' said Doug.

'After seeing that fire last week and how yer crew dealt with it, if we can help prevent that happening I'm all for it,' said Dave.

'That's marvellous,' said Roger.

'Back to the reception,' said Les.

'Not sure on that one,' said Dave.

'Well, they go hand in hand really. If we didn't acknowledge your bravery we would be crucified and accused of using you,' said Roger.

'Yes the press, local politicians and the general public would have a field day,' said James.

'I can believe that,' said Doug.

'Firstly, it is our wish to award you, what you did can never be taken lightly, bravery in whatever form, going beyond normal duty, we have to honour it,' said Roger. 'Your family, friends, anyone you wish, within reason, will be invited. It will be a small gathering of invited guests. A lunch will be served, followed by a small ceremony where you will receive our brigade certificate. I can promise you it will be done with your approval. Do you agree, lads?' said Roger.

After a short pause, Doug agreed. Moments later Dave agreed, to the elation of everyone and handshakes all round.

'I don't think you'll regret this,' said Les.

'I thought you were a little hesitant about the award, Dave,' said Roger.

'I was, I really was, but it's not about me. And, one thing I do know, I realise just how dedicated yer three in this room are, the importance this poster work is to yer fire service... so how can I stand in your way. We have to give it our full support.'

'Get yer frock out, Mum, yer going to a party.'

'Who, is?' said Helen.

'We're all going, Mrs. T.,' said Dave.

'Nan, Granddad George.'

'Where?' asked Helen.

'Town hall, next Friday,' said Doug.

'Town hall, don't see any parties in there,' said Helen.

'They have a function room on the first floor,' said Dave.

'Well, I never. Can I tell Mum and Dad?'

'No, not yet. It's not official, so yer can't say anything to anyone until we say so.'

'Have to buy a new dress. And, hat, shoes. Got to all match. And, handbag.'

'Going to be busy, Mrs T.'

'That went well,' said Les. 'I'll get James to give you a tour of the station. Are you happy with the way negotiations went?'

'Very good,' said Doug.

'Excellent,' said Dave.

'I've got the list of people you want invited. Now, the invites will be ready tomorrow and I will see you for the photo shoot in the morning. Because we are short of time, is it possible for you to hand the invites out personally?'

'That's all right,' said Doug.

'These people know already, do they?' asked Les.

'Most do, and are sworn to secrecy, for now.'

'Good, you've done well. Here's James now. I will see you bright and early tomorrow. Can you show them around please, James?'

'Here's your coffee dear,' said Grace, as she sat down opposite Charles. 'What was it you wanted to tell me, love?' asked Grace.

'We've been invited to lunch on Friday.'

'Lunch?'

'Yes, invited to an award ceremony at the town hall, for those two local lads who saved the child in that terrible fire.'

'Oh, marvellous. How lovely and well deserved,' said Grace.

'I agree,' said Charles.

'Why have we been invited?' asked Grace.

'Because of our business status,' said Charles.

'Now, just a minute, you undersell yourself every time, Charles. You do so much for the community, unsung, for many years and I'll be proud of you come Friday. I can't wait,' said Grace.

'Make a nice change,' said Charles.

'Thought you were going to say Dennis has caught someone.'

'No, Dennis told me yesterday that despite extensive investigations, they are still no nearer. And those above want to know why he's spending so much money and man hours on this inquiry, but he feels ours may not be the only one carried out.'

'Oh dear,' said Grace.

'Anyway. I'm off to work. You have a nice day, my dear, see you later,' he said as he gave her a kiss on the cheek.

CHAPTER 15
THE CEREMONY

'Yer looking beautiful, Mum.'

'Yes, you do,' said Mavis.

'Stunning Mrs T.,' said Dave.

'Thank you, I've got butterflies,' said Helen.

'The limo's turned up,' said Doug.

'Limo?' said Mavis.

'Wow. Look at that limousine,' said George.

They all gathered by the window, looking out. 'Oh, my word. Are we going in that?' asked Helen, as people came in all directions to gather outside.

'If yer all ready, then let's go,' said Doug.

'Yer scrubbed up well, Knowall.'

'Don't look bad yerself, Hobbly.'

'Got to make an effort,' said Dave.

As soon as they stepped outside the door, cheering started. As Doug helped them into the limo, the chauffeur asked if they were ready.

'Take yer time, not in any hurry,' said Doug, waving at the

people as they drove away. Alas, it didn't take long to cover the short distance, even though the driver took a detour.

The chauffeur opened the car door, where they were greeted by Roger Lee in uniform and the town's mayor, with his splendid chain, accompanied by the lady mayoress. Just beyond they noticed, in Sunday best, Maurice, Bob, Pete, Tony, Len and Glenda, ascending the stairs. After the formal greeting was concluded, they were escorted up to the main function room, where they received a rousing reception from gathered guests, before being shown to allotted places. There were eight round tables each seating six people.

On table one there was Helen, Doug, Dave, Roger, the mayor and mayoress. On table two, George, Mavis, Charles, Grace, Councillor Vine and Mrs Vine, and on table three there was Len, Glenda, Maurice, Tony, Bob and Pete.

The other tables were taken up by local dignitaries, business people and representatives of fire, police and health services. Aside from family, Doug and Dave decided to invite just six friends, the reason being, not to favour some and disappoint others. The six invited would not cause any resentment, whatsoever. Wine flowed, the meal was enjoyed and the company engaging. Now, for the presentation. Dave and Doug were given an ear bashing by Helen, not to drink too much. 'Are you OK, Mum?'

'Yes'sh,' she replied.

Roger and the mayor left the table and walked towards a stage, climbing six steps in the process, before standing behind a microphone on a stand in the centre of the stage. Roger stepped forward.

'Ladies and gentlemen. I wish to thank you for coming along today, particularly as it was at such short notice. I also wish to thank the caterers for a wonderful lunch and excellent service.' Applause all round. 'Now, I have the honour of introducing two wonderful young men, who as you will have seen, performed an act of outstanding bravery. They will each receive a framed certificate, unique to the fire service, from His Honour the Mayor. It's my pleasure to introduce David Harris and Douglas Thomas. Please come forward.'

Loud applause and cheers followed, as the two made their way forward. Charles rose to his feet, clapping along with others. He was standing directly in line with Dave as he climbed the six steps.

'That's him, that's him,' he mumbled.

'Sorry, did you say something?' asked Mavis.

'Er, no, no,' replied Charles, as he stood transfixed.

'Are you OK, Charles?' whispered Grace, to no response. 'Charles, dear?'

'Sorry love, did you say something?'

'Are you OK?'

'Yes, fine, little emotional,' said Charles, as he gently squeezed her hand. For the next few minutes he was unable to comprehend exactly what was going on. Instead his eyes didn't leave Dave. He kept re-running the walk up the steps over and over in his head. The slight limp, precise gait, prominent hip movement and the contour of his body, all seen in a combined movement. The exact same as the man he'd seen on the grass slope. It's him, it's got to be him, he kept telling himself. His thoughts were broken by applause, in which be unconsciously joined in. At this point he saw the two heading towards him. Doug passed George, who shook his hand. Mavis grabbed him and gave him a cuddle. Dave finished the conversation with the mayor as he stood feet away from Charles.

'Congratulations, Dave,' said George as he patted him on the shoulder.

'Glad that's over,' said Dave.

Charles attempted to say something, but was unable to speak.

'Congratulations, well done,' said Grace, as Dave passed by.

Doug escaped the grip of Mavis. 'Here Mum, look after this,' said Doug as he handed her the frame, giving her a kiss on the cheek.

'Cour'sh I will, shun,' said Helen.

'How lovely,' said Grace.

'Ladies and gentlemen. If you will please take your seats I have one more announcement to make,' Roger looked behind and saw Les and James in position, they nodded in his direction. 'OK, ladies and gentlemen. As you can see, behind me is a poster, covered with a white sheet, I can now reveal our poster boys for the fire prevention week,' he nodded as the sheet slowly fell to the floor, 'are... David Harris and Douglas Thomas.'

A loud applause broke out, as the poster showed the life size photos of Dave and Doug in full firemen's uniform, with a roll of hosepipe draped over their shoulders. Roger continued, 'I wish to thank both these young men for agreeing to take part in this campaign, it will save lives, many lives, by making people aware of the dangers. Thank you all.'

So ended an enjoyable ceremony; the successful launch of the poster campaign, the propelling of two young men into the limelight of public attention and the unknowing prospect of it crashing down.

'I've made coffee,' said Charles.

'Thank you. That was a lovely lunch, I so enjoyed it,' said Grace. She sat at the kitchen table and kicked off her shoes. 'You seemed a little subdued during the ceremony,' said Grace.

Charles handed her a cup of coffee, then sat down opposite her. 'I think I know the name of the man who robbed our company,' said Charles.

'Pardon?' said Grace.

'Yes, I think I know.'

'Darling. Have you informed Dennis?'

'No, not yet,' replied Charles.

'Well, you must,' said Grace, taking a sip of coffee.

'Do you think so?' asked Charles.

'Of course, when did you find out?'

'Today,' replied Charles.

'You're being a bit coy, Charles, what is it?'

'Do you want to know the man's name?'

'Yes, of course.'

'It's David Harris.'

'You're kidding me!'

He explained his reasoning behind the accusation.

'Oh my God, Charles!' Grace sat in stunned silence. After a short pause, she asked. 'What do you intend to do?'

Charles shook his head slowly. 'I don't know, love. We need to work out what's best.'

'I understand,' said Grace.

'The correct course of action would be to tell Dennis,' said Charles.

'I agree,' said Grace. 'But by doing that, we destroy David. What a dilemma,' said Grace.

'Even to be charged with this crime could finish him. It would damage the poster campaign, for sure,' said Charles.

'If he were to be charged, then found guilty, he's destroyed,' said Grace.

'Do we seek justice for the crime committed or do we look at compassion?' asked Charles.

'Ideally we could have both, but we know full well we can only have one or the other,' said Grace.

'You're right, love. It's one or the other.'

'Let me tell you how I'm thinking. If he were sent to prison, it would be for punishment, as well as rehabilitation. I just think he's already started his rehabilitation. Firstly, with the heroics during the fire, then the poster campaign, I'm for punishment fitting the crime when you do wrong, but under these circumstances I'm against destroying him.'

'Fair enough,' said Charles. 'I must take those valid views into account, against my firm belief that when you knowingly commit a crime, you must pay a price. I think it best if I sleep on it and I suggest you do the same.'

'I better get Mum some coffee. Anyone else?'

'I'll have one,' said George.

'Me too,' said Mavis.

'Did you have a good time, Mrs. T.?'

'Marvell'oush,' said Helen as she went through to the lounge.

'First time I've ever seen her like that,' said Mavis.

'Did you enjoy it, George?'

'Yeah, brilliant. Good Company as well. Charles is in business but nothing stuck up about them two, lovely people.'

'Who was he?' asked Dave.

'Charles White of Whites Engineering.'

'No!' said Dave, with a look of surprise.

'Yeah, what a lovely man,' said Mavis.

'Well I never,' said Dave.

'Did you know him then?' asked George.

'No, heard of him though,' replied Dave.

'Here's your coffee.' Doug put a tray on the table. 'I think Mum's nodded off, look at her. Can't believe that she gave us a lecture about drinking too much today. I told her to ease up on the wine. Trouble was, she was drinking red and white, that can be lethal when yer not use to it,' said Doug.

'What we doing later?' asked Dave.

'I think I'm gonna have to keep an eye on her. Got a few cans in the fridge. And a couple of cases, just in case anyone came back. Tell yer what, I'll ring round to see if we can get a card school going, what do yer reckon?'

'Sounds good to me,' said Dave.

CHAPTER 16
THE CONCLUSION

'Good morning, love.'

'Morning dear, what would you like for breakfast?' asked Grace.

'I'll have something later, if you don't mind.'

'Would you like tea?'

'Yes please, I'll be in the lounge,' said Charles.

Minutes later she gave Charles his tea, before sitting down next to him on a large settee. 'You didn't sleep very well,' said Grace.

'No, not sure you did either.'

'No I didn't. Mulling it over for most of the night,' said Grace.

'You would think it easy to come to decision. Anything but,' said Charles.

'For the sake of argument, let's presume that David Harris was the man you saw. If we agree that, then it's clear; give his name to Dennis,' said Grace.

'If he was eventually found guilty, he would serve a prison

sentence, so depriving him of his liberty,' said Charles.

'Some would say Justice done,' said Grace.

'So, what's your conclusion, Grace?'

'Difficult. But I just favour him carrying on as it is, without exposing him. And, you Charles?'

'Like you Grace, I find it difficult. Lots of to-ing and fro-ing.'

'Let's say he's out in three years after serving a prison sentence. He comes out, all repentant for what he did. He's rehabilitated. So, then he looks for work but due to his criminal record he finds it hard to get a job. So, it's likely to take a long time before he's successful in doing so. I don't think it right that I put him through an uncertain future, just for me to be able to say he's been punished.'

'I totally agreed with you, Grace, when you put it so well. He's already turned his life round and that's good enough for me. Even though we are breaking the law by shielding him.'

'I'm with you, Charles, it's the right decision, come what may. One other thing that helped persuade me was the fact he is taking part in a campaign that will save lives, many lives. He wouldn't be doing much of that in prison.'

DAVID HARRIS

went from strength to strength, never diverting from the straight and narrow. Other opportunities opened up for him and Doug and he's come a long way from the school tuckshop boy with sticky fingers.

DOUGLAS THOMAS

continued to prosper, along with Dave, still living at home with Mum, Helen, who incidentally hasn't touched a drop since. As for his aunt Vi: Bristol 1 Aunt Vi 2.

PETER WALKER.

is doing well, working for Malcolm and his dad in the undertaking business, although his mates reckon it's a bit of a dead-end job. He's 6'4", so when they carry the coffin it tends to look a little lopsided.

MAURICE FORD

Business is booming for Oilrag. But, furniture removal is not part of his present day business. There's only one Oilrag.

TONY BOND

might be the first of the lads to fly the nest. He's got engaged. He's known as Orange because he's tight fisted. Question. Who's paying for the wedding, if it happens, and what sort of engagement ring is it… a curtain ring?

BOB WILSON

He's always had a passion for food. Perhaps that's one reason why he's now a manager at McDonald's, the food closest to his heart. If it were a choice of a good woman or a McDonald's, then it's 'nice knowing you, lady' and 'welcome burger and chip's'.

GRANDAD GEORGE

He had to revise his view of his grandson. George was not one to admit he got it wrong, but losers' was no longer appropriate for Dave or his mates.

His grandson went from zero to hero. If only he knew the truth they'd be propelled to 'BORN BLEEDIN' LOSERS'.

THE END